Goddess Girls

MEDEA
THE
ENCHANTRESS

Goddess Girls

MEDEA THE ENCHANTRESS

JOAN HOLUB & SUZANNE WILLIAMS

Aladdin

NEW YORK   LONDON   TORONTO   SYDNEY   NEW DELHI

An imprint of Simon & Schuster Children's Publishing Division
1230 Avenue of the Americas, New York, New York 10020
First Aladdin paperback edition December 2017
Text copyright © 2017 by Joan Holub and Suzanne Williams
Cover illustration copyright © 2017 by Glen Hanson
Also available in an Aladdin hardcover edition.
All rights reserved, including the right of reproduction in whole or in part in any form.
ALADDIN and related logo are registered trademarks of Simon & Schuster, Inc.
For information about special discounts for bulk purchases, please contact
Simon & Schuster Special Sales at 1-866-506-1949 or business@simonandschuster.com.
The Simon & Schuster Speakers Bureau can bring authors to your live event.
For more information or to book an event contact the Simon & Schuster Speakers Bureau
at 1-866-248-3049 or visit our website at www.simonspeakers.com.
Book designed by Karin Paprocki
The text of this book was set in Baskerville.
Manufactured in the United States of America 1117 OFF
2 4 6 8 10 9 7 5 3 1
Library of Congress Control Number 2017937867
ISBN 978-1-4814-7018-6 (hc)
ISBN 978-1-4814-7017-9 (pbk)
ISBN 978-1-4814-7019-3 (eBook)

We appreciate our mega-amazing readers!

*Andrade Family, Olivia H., Kaylee S., Marisa H.,
Brienna J., Alexis T., Emily and Grondine Family,
McKenna A., Caitlin R., Hannah R., Paris O., Kira L.,
Haley G., Riley G., Renee G., Lillia L., Haidi S.,
Keny Y., Koko Y., Micci S., Brianna I.,
McKenna W., Audrey H., Amelia G.,
Ally M., Keyra M., Sabrina C., Gracie J., Leah R.,
McKay O., Reese O., Christine D-H., Khanya S.,
Olivia C., Annie S., Tia S., Madison W., Amya L.,
Virginia J., Shelby J., Samantha J., Kristen S.,
Kiana Layla E., Lana W., Iida L., Stephanie T.,
Kaitlyn W., Hallie F., Sidney F., Buu Buu,
Caroline T., Ava F., Tamsin H., Kassondra N.,
Shannon D., Fe Susan D., Sarah May D.,
Patricia Jennifer D., Malia C., Ana Carolina G.,
Ella C., Jenny C., Lorelai M., Brynn S., Jorja S.,
Alexa R., Samantha K., Caitlynn L., Arianna O.,
Alex B., Jimena C., Stephanie R., Adriana V., Gia W.,
Paige J., Megan D., Rachel B., Danielle H., Barbara E.,
Emily E., Virginia J., Shelby J., Samatha J., and you!*

—J. H. and S. W.

CONTENTS

Goddess Girls

MEDEA
THE
ENCHANTRESS

1

Danger!

TWELVE-YEAR-OLD MEDEA TWIRLED A LOCK OF her long black hair around a gold-tipped laurel-wood wand. Her wand was magic. A standard school supply, it had been issued to her at Enchantment Academy earlier in the year. With each twirl of the wand, streaks of rainbow sparkles zinged from its tip through her hair. And each time she unwound the curl from her wand, the streaks quickly faded to black again.

However, as she sat on a window seat in the throne room of her father's palace in the land of Colchis on the Black Sea, Medea didn't notice any of this. Instead, her blue eyes were glued to the scroll in her lap. It was last week's issue of *Teen Scrollazine*. On Friday she had traded her lunch money for it to a girl at school named Glauce. (Totally worth it!) It was Sunday night now, and all weekend Medea had been sneaking around here at home, reading the 'zine in secret.

Not only was *T-zine* full of fashion advice and news stories, it contained a column penned by Pheme, the goddessgirl of gossip. Her column was all about the exploits of the gods and goddesses of Mount Olympus. And it was especially delicious this week!

It seemed that Aphrodite, the goddessgirl of love and beauty, had worn painted bronze accessories with one of her dazzling pink chitons recently, setting off a new fashion craze among mortals on Earth. Also, Eros, the godboy of love, was testing out mini-size versions of his magic crush-causing arrows. And if Pheme had her facts straight, some students in a class called Hero-ology, which was taught by Mr. Cyclops at Mount Olympus Academy, would soon embark on a mysterious, heroic adventure!

Suddenly Medea's head popped up like she was a rabbit scenting danger. Footsteps! And voices! King Aeëtes (her dad) and Circe (her aunt) were coming her way! With a quick wave of her wand, she caused the window seat's curtains to magically whip shut around it, closing her off from the rest of the room. There was no telling what her dad would do if he caught her reading the 'zine.

He had strict rules, and he disapproved of *Teen*

Scrollazine big-time. He only wanted her to read things that made her "smarter." Which he claimed gossip didn't. Maybe not, but in her opinion Pheme's column was a lot of fun. And shouldn't reading be fun? Often the reading material her dad *did* approve of (hello, encyclopedia scrolls?) wasn't.

Besides, there was other stuff in the 'zine too. A few weeks ago there had even been an article about her dad's amazing cape. The one he'd nicknamed the Golden Fleece. But even that article—which had been stuffed with facts—hadn't impressed him. Still, everyone she knew practically devoured the stories in the 'zine. If she didn't do the same, she wouldn't know what they were talking about at school on Monday!

Stomp, stomp! Tap, tap! The two sets of footsteps stopped right outside the window seat where she sat.

Medea held the 'zine against her chest and tried not to breathe too loudly.

"I've had a vision. Danger is coming," she heard her aunt Circe say in that special faraway voice she used when she was telling a prophecy. Not only was she Medea's aunt, she was also one of the greatest sorceresses of all time and the principal of Enchantment Academy, where Medea attended school.

The king's voice tightened. "Explain."

Medea heard the jangle of bracelets and knew her typically dramatic aunt must be waving her hands expressively as she announced, "A thief will soon come to Colchis to steal your Golden Fleece!"

Medea's eyes rounded and she let out a tiny gasp. Luckily, her dad snorted at the same time, covering the sound she'd made.

"Probably thanks to the article in that blabby *Teen Scrollazine* telling the world about it!" said the king. "But the serpent-dragon I have guarding the fleece should stop any thief. I'm not worried."

Medea's gaze shot to the windowpane behind her. In a distant part of the realm she could see green puffs of smoke rising into the air. They were coming from the fiery snout of the very dragon her father spoke of. One that never slept and always prowled around the sacred grove where the fleece hung, unblinkingly keeping guard on it. The serpent-dragon obeyed her father faithfully and no one else.

A ray of sunlight fell upon the fleece where it hung from the grove's largest and most splendid oak tree. The picture of a fierce-looking ram's head that was embroidered on it with golden thread momentarily gleamed like fire. That cape was cool, she had to admit. It was woven from the wool (aka fleece) of a rare and famous ram (a male sheep). Her dad displayed the fleece on a high branch outdoors in order to honor its origins as a wild animal.

The king only wore his fleece cape on super-duper special occasions, but he adored it so much that he went to visit it every day. He'd even had a jeweled chair set below it so he could sit and admire the cape for as long as he wanted. Sometimes Medea thought he loved that fleece more than her!

"That's not all," Circe went on now. "This thief will be a handsome boy who will steal the heart of your daughter as well."

At this information Medea whipped her head toward the sound of their voices again. *Handsome boy?* She scooched quietly across the window seat cushion and parted the curtains a crack with the tip of her wand, just in time to see her dad frown.

"What? Medea's only twelve. Much too young to be thinking about boys," he huffed.

Circe arched an eyebrow at him. "Some girls her age do get crushes, you know. Not all, but some."

Her dad sliced his hand through the air, shaking his head in his usual bossy, kingly way. "Medea's not going to go on her first date till she's eighteen. No, make that *thirty* years old. I won't allow it."

"Don't be ridiculous. And I didn't say she would be going on dates anytime soon. I said she might get a crush," said Circe. "She's growing up whether you like it or not."

"Ha! Well, maybe I'll just put out a proclamation that any boy caught within a mile of my daughter will be jailed! That'll put a stop to any heart stealing." Looking pleased with this solution, yet still a little worried, the king turned to go.

However Circe's next words stopped him. "Even an extreme measure like that is unlikely to prevent my prophecy from coming true." The king whirled toward her, frowny faced again. Before he could interrupt, she rushed on. "Listen, brother, I have an idea. I've been invited to substitute-teach a class at Mount Olympus Academy this coming week. I could use a couple of student assistants. Since danger is looming here, why don't you let me take Medea away to safety at MOA?"

Ooh! This is reeeally getting interesting! thought Medea. Danger was coming. She might get to go to MOA with her aunt. How exciting! *And* a crush? Well, she wasn't that into liking boys, but whatever. She didn't have to crush on anyone she didn't want to, no matter what appeared in Circe's visions, right?

Rising to her knees on the cushion, she angled her head for a better view of her dad's face. Her aunt was one of those cool grown-ups who "got" kids and let them have fun, within reason. But one look at her dad's expression, and her hopes of going on an adventure to the school attended by awesome immortals like Aphrodite and Pheme were pretty much dashed.

"Medea go with you? I don't think so," the king said, scoffing at the idea. "I would trust no one—not even you—to guard the princess of this kingdom in a place so far away. I might let her visit MOA someday, but only after I'm certain that her magic skills have been perfected to a point where she can protect herself, or at least not embarrass our realm."

Medea felt her cheeks burn. Her dad treated her like a little kid sometimes! His rules for her were way stricter than those he had for his royal subjects. He was always trying to control her every move, forever bossing her around. "Go here! Do this! Don't do that! Get your homework done! No reading *Teen Scrollazine*!" At least, that's how it seemed to her.

He wouldn't let her hang out with kids he didn't approve of either, and he wouldn't let her board at the Academy like everyone else did. She was the only student enrolled at EA who had to travel to and from home. That meant a half hour of travel by wand magic from Colchis way over to the Academy on Aeaea Island and back. Every. Single. Day. Not only was that a big pain logistically, it also meant she had zero chance of being one of the students invited to join the Magicasters Club in the upcoming annual tryouts. Because that club met after school, while she was here at home in Colchis.

"If you don't give your daughter any freedom to make her own mistakes, she'll never learn how to take care of herself," Circe argued.

"Exactly my point. My precious little girl is still a baby in many ways. It's my job to protect her since she cannot take care of herself. We don't want her burning MOA down with those eyes of hers, do we? Zeus might not take kindly to that!"

Medea's fingers fisted, one hand clenching her wand and her other crunching the scrollazine she still held. *Grr.* She squinched her eyes shut so they wouldn't flash and give her hiding place away. Or cause a fire hazard! The granddaughter of the sun god Helios, she'd been born with eyes that flashed fiery-hot, golden light rays whenever she felt strong negative emotions. Like now, when she was totally and completely annoyed by her dad!

Or like the time when she was four years old and some mean kids made off with a pile of seashells she'd been collecting on the beach. She glared at those kids so hard, they got sunburns. Most people thought they'd just been out in the sun too long that day, but Medea's dad and aunt knew better. After that, they watched her closely and made rules.

Still, they couldn't watch her all the time, and well, sometimes people just stressed her out or made her mega-mad! After the sunburn incident there had been the tomato incident back in first grade. That had sort of been her classmate Glauce's fault, though. And it had marked the beginning of Medea secretly nicknaming that girl her "frenemy." Because that term meant "a person who sometimes acts like a friend and other times acts like an enemy." Which described Glauce 100 percent!

Not wanting to think about that horrible tomato incident right now, Medea gave her head a shake to clear it and then went back to eavesdropping.

"I'm only saying that maybe you should allow Medea to fall on her face a few times. Let her suffer the consequences of her mistakes," she heard her aunt say. "She'll learn from it."

Yeah, Dad. It's only for a week. Let me fall on my face if I want to, Medea whispered, but only in her mind. She didn't really think anything bad would happen if she got to go to MOA with her aunt. Happy scenes of just the opposite filled her head. If she did get the chance, she promised herself she wouldn't trip up. Instead she would find a way to make a fabulous impression on the immortals who went to school there. And news of her success would find its way back to her dad. She smiled dreamily, imagining his proud face when that happened.

"Don't forget that if you let her go to MOA, you might be able to thwart the heart-stealing part of my vision. Which might prevent the fleece-stealing part from coming true as well," coaxed Circe.

Her dad scowled at her aunt. "I said no, and that's final!" he roared.

Stomp, stomp! Tap, tap! Her father's and aunt's footsteps faded from the room as they exited it and moved down the hall. Medea parted the curtains a tad wider and held her ear to the opening, listening for more.

"I'm not going to let this go!" Circe was insisting.

Score! thought Medea upon hearing this. Because her aunt was very good at getting her way. Once it was quiet, Medea leaped from her hiding place.

When her red lace-up sandals touched the floor, she did a little happy dance out of the throne room. Then, all the way down the long, marble-tiled hall to her bedroom, she waved the rolled-up 'zine like a parade leader with a baton.

Confident of Circe's ability to eventually persuade her dad, she decided to go pack her sleepover things and pick out the perfect accessories to wear with her school uniform tomorrow. Because she had a feeling she would almost certainly be traveling on from EA to Mount Olympus! If she could do something while there to make her dad proud, then maybe, just maybe, he'd stop being so bossy. And after she came back from MOA, he might even agree to let her board at Enchantment Academy and just come home on school breaks or on weekends like other kids. That way, she'd have a chance at joining the Magicasters Club after all! *Squee!*

As she came to a stop before her wardrobe and began going through her stuff, she recalled her aunt saying that she could use a *couple* of assistants. *Hmm.* Which other student from EA would Circe choose to go with them?

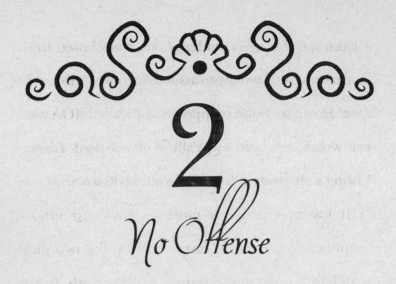

2
No Offense

N O OFFENSE, BUT YOU REALLY SHOULDN'T HOLD
your magic wand that way," said a fake-sweet voice.
"It's dangerous. Remember the exploding tomato
incident?"

Medea winced and glanced at the speaker—the
pretty, blond Glauce. Her *frenemy*. Even though her
dad had (reluctantly) agreed to let his baby come
to Mount Olympus Academy, it turned out that

Glauce was the other student Circe had chosen from Enchantment Academy to assist her here all this week. *Drat!* How was Medea supposed to shine at MOA with the wonderful and magically accomplished Glauce casting a shadow of greatness over her?

It was now Monday morning, and just fifteen minutes ago Circe had cast a spell on the two girls that had caused their wands to glow with travel magic. This had whisked Glauce and Medea from EA to MOA, where they now stood in the middle of a group of students about their age in the Hero-ology classroom.

Of course I recall the tomato incident, Medea thought as everyone awaited Circe's arrival. (Her aunt had sent the girls on before her.) How could she forget, with Glauce reminding her every school year since they were six years old?

Here's what happened that awful day: Medea had been holding her magic wand in preparation for doing her first "spell-casting test on faraway things." She'd been calm and ready.

But then Glauce had said something like, "Good luck. Don't mess up like you usually do." It was that kind of half-nice, half-mean comment that was typical of this confusing girl. And it had gotten Medea so rattled and unsure that she had mixed up the wand positions.

Splat! She'd caused the tomato, a target that sat way across the classroom by the teacher's desk, to blow up instead of grow up to pumpkin size as she'd intended. The explosion had spattered bright orange-red goo and seeds all over the teacher and a few of her classmates, too.

But why did Glauce have to go and bring that

up now? In front of two dozen or so immortal and mortal students at MOA, no less! They had all turned to look at the two girls when they first appeared.

And now to make things worse, Glauce reached over and repositioned Medea's wand while everyone in class was still staring. "There, that's better. First is resting position," Glauce said in satisfaction, after angling Medea's wand from third position to first.

There were five proper angles at which to hold a wand, and Glauce was right that first was the safest way to keep your wand from accidentally doing magic. In first position you grasped a wand in your fist with its magic-tip end pointing down between your third and fourth fingers.

However, third position, where you held the wand like a pencil with thumb and index finger on top and the wand resting on your middle finger, was considered almost as safe. It was a neutral position that allowed a wand's powers to be in gear and at the ready. And you never knew when you might need to use your magic, right?

Medea felt like reminding Glauce of that. Instead she heard herself give a nervous giggle, then say, "Thanks. Wouldn't want to cause another boom-in-the-room or a tomato volcano or a—"

"Okay, okay, enough. Stop embarrassing us in front of these immortals," said Glauce, rolling her eyes at Medea's lame-o jokes. She fluffed her curly blond hair with one hand and smiled around at the curious onlookers.

Medea stared down at her wand, turning it around and around in her hands. It was kind of humiliating to be scolded in front of these strangers she'd so wanted to impress. She should've known Glauce would be the other assistant chosen for this trip, though. Her frenemy was the best student in their Wand-Waving class and a shoo-in to be invited into the supercool Magicasters Club during next week's tryouts. Medea knew she should be grateful for her suggestions. It was just that the *way* Glauce offered those suggestions could be *sooo* annoying!

Still, she didn't dare offend the girl. For some reason Glauce had decided to include her in her circle of popular friends, and Medea didn't want to get on her bad side. Besides, there were times when Glauce could be a real pal. Like once when Medea had forgotten her wand at home during fourth-grade finals and Glauce used her travel magic to fetch it. Yet at other times this girl seemed to purposely look for ways to put her down.

Whoosh! Suddenly a woman-size tornado appeared in the classroom doorway in a swirl of long red hair, a dress draped with veils, and tons of showy jewelry. Circe had arrived! After coming to an abrupt stop, she flung the cape she carried aside with a dramatic flourish and favored the Hero-ology students with a simple bow of her head.

"Good morning, class! I'm Sorceress Circe, principal of Enchantment Academy. I hope you haven't been up to any mischief with your teacher away. Not without me here to enjoy the fun, at any rate." Her merry laughter rang out, causing students to smile.

"She sure knows how to make an entrance," murmured a goddessgirl standing near Medea. She had gray-blue eyes and wore a blue chiton. And even though her long, wavy brown hair was done up in a high twist held in place by a small stick of polished wood, Medea recognized her right off. The brainy Athena! Her dad was Zeus, King of the Gods and Ruler of the Heavens, as well as principal of MOA.

Standing alongside Athena was a beautiful golden-haired goddessgirl dressed in pink and wearing a chunky painted bronze bracelet and matching necklace. Definitely Aphrodite. These two were among the most popular goddessgirls at MOA! As with all immortals, their skin looked like it had been lightly powdered with delicate sparkles of glitter that glinted when the light hit them just so. Medea had heard about that phenomenon, but it was amazing to see it for herself.

"Yeah, I *love* her style!" Aphrodite agreed with Athena. Casually gesturing toward Medea, who was directly in the two goddessgirls' line of sight, Aphrodite added, "And those Enchantment Academy uniforms are really fab." Medea and Glauce were wearing the official uniform of their school—a red chiton edged with gold trim and emblazoned with the swirly gold EA logo. Medea had accessorized with her favorite braided gold belt, matching ruby-studded gold hair hoop, and gold lace-up sandals.

When Medea smiled at Aphrodite and Athena, the two girls smiled back. Noticing this interaction, Glauce stepped in front of Medea and smiled at the girls too.

"Class?" When Circe spoke just then, all eyes turned her way. "Many of you may already know that Mr. Cyclops is away at Giant-Con, a convention of giants on the island of Hypereia." As she spoke, she wound her way grandly around the room, her dress and veils fluttering out behind her like sails, even though there was no wind. "During his absence this week I'll be substitute-teaching all Hero-ology classes. Today each class will begin a different group quest that will end on Friday."

Hearing this short deadline, some students gasped. Then a boy with turquoise eyes said, "I bet this will be the adventure Pheme wrote about in *Teen Scrollazine*!" The two godboys beside him nodded and looked over at a girl with short orange hair and small, glittery orange wings. A tiny thrill zinged through Medea. Because this was surely Pheme, the goddessgirl of gossip herself!

And the boy who had spoken had to be Poseidon, godboy of the sea! Medea recognized him from drawings in *Teen Scrollazine*, as well as from the three-pronged pitchfork-like trident he held. His two godboy buds she could also identify from pictures in past issues of *Teen Scrollazine*. They were Apollo, godboy of prophecy and music among other things, and Ares, the godboy of war.

Medea grinned to herself. Happy she was able to recognize so many faces, she thought: *See, Dad? Stuff you see in* Teen Scrollazine *can come in handy!*

"Yes, it's not much time," Circe continued, having heard the students' concerned gasps. "Things will move at a quick pace this week, with lots of events requiring magic. For anything advanced you may come to me. For instances where simple magic is required, you may consult my two able assistants and enchantresses in training, Medea and Glauce." Circe's many bracelets and rings flashed as she gestured in the direction of the two girls.

Medea smiled and gave a shy little wave to everyone. However, Glauce bowed, waving her wand with a grand flourish that left a sparkly trail of letters hanging in midair. Letters that spelled: HI, MOA!

Why didn't I think of doing something spectacular like that? wondered Medea. Because she wasn't as socially confident as Glauce, that's why. Nor as showy. Her frenemy's move had been perfectly planned to impress.

Feeling like she'd totally bombed in some kind of unspoken contest, Medea tried to make up for her earlier lack of coolness by imitating Glauce. Even as she bowed and waved her wand to leave a trail of her own sparkly letters, Medea knew that copying was the wrong thing to do. She wasn't Glauce. She should just be herself. How many times had her aunt told her that?

As Medea straightened again, Glauce lifted an eyebrow at her and made a tsking sound. "Really?" she said, glancing toward Medea's trail of letters.

Oh no! Medea's heart plummeted when she looked

over too. In her anxious rush she'd misspelled her sparkle message as HI, MOO!

"Oops," she said. Luckily, the letters faded quickly. But not before most of the class had seen them, she guessed from the quiet giggles that ran through the room. She had hoped to leave a great impression here at MOA. And right off the bat she'd totally bungled!

Not seeming to notice anything amiss, Circe spread her arms wide, bracelets jangling. "Let's get to it! Now, I understand from Mr. Cyclops that you completed an assignment earlier this year in which you guided certain mortal heroes—including the famous Odysseus—on some Earth adventures. In this week's project you'll help another great hero attempt to cross a dangerous sea. And what does a sailor need to go on a heroic voyage?"

"A ship!" Athena called out.

"A crew!" shouted Apollo.

"Good answers! And that's where all of you come in," said Circe, clapping her hands in delight. "This morning you'll each be assigned a new hero who will be part of the great heroic leader's crew. Mr. Cyclops left little hero statues for us somewhere in this classroom," she said, glancing around. "As soon as I locate them and pass them out, we'll move ahead. For now, students, please start removing your old heroes from the game board to make room." So saying, Circe motioned toward the Ping-Pong-size table in the middle of the floor. The "game board," Medea figured.

Looking around, Medea saw that some of the students were gazing at her a bit uncertainly. Had her mistakes with wand holding and introducing herself with a *MOO* caused them to doubt her ability as an enchantress? Probably. And Glauce's scoffing reactions to those mistakes undoubtedly hadn't helped. She felt sure the immortals would all ignore her and flock to Glauce if they needed tips or had questions this week. Frustration welled up inside her. Jealousy, too.

Truth was, Medea had long envied Glauce's magical abilities, though she wasn't a bit proud of that fact. If envy were a wart or a bruise, she would remove it from herself with a tap of her magic wand. Unfortunately, wands couldn't remove feelings.

While Circe began searching Mr. Cyclops's desk drawers and supply closet shelves for the new hero statues, Medea headed across the room. Maybe some immortals over by that game board table hadn't noticed her wand-spelling error and already written her off as an idiot. Or else decided she'd intended to insult them by calling them a bunch of cows. (HI, MOO!) *Argh!*

A huge, realistic-looking three-dimensional map covered the table's entire surface, Medea saw once she went closer. She walked around the table, studying the map's features.

There were roads, villages, and castles with moats around them. And labeled by name were various countries, islands, and seas. The tallest mountain stood nearly a foot high, and the oceans and seas had actual moving waves with strange, scaly beasts peeking from them. She dipped the tip end of her wand into the Mediterranean Sea, testing its depth. Instantly a real sea monster about six inches long leaped from the water. It momentarily twined around her wand, then let go and splashed back into the sea!

She gasped in surprise. "Mega-cool!"

"I know, isn't it?" said the goddessgirl Athena, who'd come up behind her. She introduced herself, though Medea already knew who she was, of course, and then said, "You're Medea, right?"

Medea smiled and nodded, then watched as Athena reached out to the game board and picked up a three-inch-tall hero statue that must have been left over from their previous assignment. The carved mortal guy in her hand wore gold sandals and a white toga, and had an adventurous gleam in his eyes.

Speaking to the statue, Athena said, "So long, Odysseus. You were the best!" Everyone on Earth knew she had greatly helped this Greek hero in fighting the Trojan War and in finding his way back home to Greece afterward. But how had she done all that from here at MOA?

"So how does this game board work exactly?" Medea asked before Athena could leave the table.

"Well, we move our hero statues around on it while trying to help them reach their goals," the goddessgirl explained. "Whatever happens to the heroes here on the board actually happens to them in real life down on Earth."

"Yeah, and we get graded on how well our hero succeeds," added Aphrodite, who'd come over too. She removed a small statue from the 3-D map as well. When she turned him to face Medea, Medea noted that Aphrodite's bronze-painted fingernails perfectly matched her stunning jewelry. She certainly lived up to her title, the goddessgirl of love and *beauty*!

"This was my hero for our first assignment. Paris, a Greek prince," Aphrodite told her.

"Paris, the guy that fell in love with Helen of Troy?" said Medea. She had learned the history of the Trojan War at school.

"Right," said Aphrodite, looking pleased that Medea had heard of her hero. She pointed at the map. "Like Athena said, whatever happens to the heroes on the board actually happens to the real-life heroes. It's kind of like a chess game, only more interesting."

"Whoa! So you guys actually get to boss around famous heroes like Odysseus and Paris?" Medea asked.

"We think of it more like *guiding* them," Athena replied.

Medea wrinkled her nose. "My dad always likes to say he's guiding me, too, when really he's bossing me around."

Apparently Athena could relate to this because she laughed with good humor. "I totally get what you're saying. My dad can be the same way!"

"Really? Zeus constantly asks if you got your homework done? And picks your friends?" Medea asked in surprise.

"Well, maybe not that, but—" began Athena.

"He does zap her friends with little thunderbolts," interrupted Aphrodite. "Not on purpose, but still. And I think he sometimes expects a lot more from her than from other students. Right, Athena?"

"I don't mind that last part," Athena mused, grinning. "But those zaps are kind of an embarrassment. As well as a real pain!"

Medea shifted from one foot to the other and remained silent. She knew all about zapping. Little did these goddessgirls know that with a flash of her eyes she could heat their entire game board so hot it would melt! But that would only happen if something or someone made her *really* upset.

"Athena! Aphrodite!" a voice suddenly gushed. Glauce had come over, and now she wedged herself between Medea and the two goddessgirls. "I have absolutely *got* to tell you how much I loved *The Iliad* and *The Odyssey*! I read both scrollbooks *three* times. Odysseus and Paris are sooo adorable. I mean, Paris played such a key role in *The Iliad*. And Odysseus was the star of both stories!"

Aphrodite smiled at Glauce, then spoke to the dark-haired prince statue she held. "You are pretty adorable, Paris. But into the cabinet you go. Nothing personal, but we're being reassigned to new heroes on a new adventure." With that, she headed across the room to set Paris on a cabinet shelf, just as other students were doing with their little statues.

Something brushed the top of Medea's head as a girl came up beside her to reach for another hero. Medea lifted a hand and found herself touching—a snake!? Along with a bunch of other snakes, it was attached to the top of the girl's head and had wiggled over to check Medea out. With pale-green skin and snakes for hair, this girl could only be the mortal MOA student Medusa!

"There you are, King Menelaus," Medusa said as she snatched a crowned statue from the game board. Now the green girl turned to Medea and Glauce. "So what else can you guys do with your wands besides spell out sparkly greetings?"

At the sight of the girl's squirming snakes, Glauce's eyes went wide and she took a quick step back. She'd always been afraid of creepy-crawly things. However, Medea wasn't. "All kinds of stuff," she answered Medusa. "Like slow things down or speed them up, or transform one thing into another. We can even cloak people and objects—make them invisible, I mean. The hardest subjects to work magic on are anything far away."

"Like how far away could your magic go?" asked Athena, cocking her head.

Medea shrugged and gestured out the nearest classroom window. "Really far. Farther than you can even see." This was true for most students. But ever since the tomato incident, she had struggled with this aspect of magic, mostly due to a lack of confidence.

"Also, our wands can transport us almost anywhere, too," Glauce added. "Good thing for Medea, since her dad won't let her board at school like every-one else, even though Principal Circe is her aunt. Poor Medea's the only one at Enchantment Academy who has to 'wand' herself to school and back home every day. A three-thousand-mile round-trip! Can you imagine?" She hugged Medea. Whether in true sympathy or just for show, Medea wasn't sure.

"Circe's your aunt?" Athena asked. She smiled at Medea's nod, then added, "Well, if your magic is anything as powerful as hers, and you decide to use it against our heroes, they had better beware. On Odysseus's trip home after the Trojan War, Circe turned his entire crew into pigs and then sent him to the Underworld for a while!"

"Yeah, I read that. Sorry! I promise—no pig transformations this time!" Medea laughed, and Athena joined in.

Glauce frowned. "Well, no offense to Medea . . . ," she began. Medea cringed. *Uh-oh!* Whenever Glauce started a sentence this way, the next thing she said would likely hurt someone's feelings. Usually Medea's! Sure enough, Glauce went on to say, "But she can't always control her magic. She should come with a warning label that says, 'Don't upset me, because you won't like what happens.'"

"So what happens?" Apollo asked Medea. He and some other guys in class had come over to remove their heroes from the map too.

Before Medea could reply, Glauce exclaimed, "She could fry you with just one look!" Then she held her fingers up near her eyes and made flicking motions to indicate zapping rays.

"Whoa! Awesome!" said Ares and Heracles, overhearing and looking impressed.

"Yeah!" Apollo nodded.

Athena looked awed as well.

"Interesting," said Medusa, giving Medea a fist bump. "Kind of similar to my stone-gaze power, then." Medea had read that Medusa could turn mortals to stone by looking directly into their eyes. Luckily for Medea, Glauce, and the mortals who attended MOA, Medusa was wearing stoneglasses today that prevented her from accidentally turning them into statues!

By now this green girl must be kind of used to her snake hair and her strange eye power making her different from other mortals. But if Medea's own weird power helped Medusa feel like less of an odd-ball, then Medea was glad of it.

Glauce looked somewhat disappointed by every-one's approval of Medea's fry power. Though pleased at that approval, Medea wanted to change the subject. Because she had a hunch the boys were about to ask for a demonstration. And her power was no joking matter!

"Aha! Here they are!" Circe called to the class.

Relieved at the interruption, Medea pointed to her aunt, who was holding a large trophy cup. "Oh, good. Looks like my aunt Circe found your new heroes!"

3

Jason

QUICKLY ATHENA, MEDUSA, AND THE BOYS hurried off to set their heroes in a cabinet along the wall like Aphrodite had. Other students who hadn't yet done so also rushed over to remove their old hero statues from the game board and stow them away.

Coming to stand in the center of the classroom now, Circe held out the trophy cup labeled FIRST-PERIOD HERO-OLOGY to show the students that it was piled high with little wooden statues. These new heroes were only about an inch tall, which was a third the size of Odysseus and the previous statues. Each had a tiny scroll attached to it by a ribbon. Four more such cups full of little heroes sat in the cabinet behind the teacher's desk, each labeled for students in the second- through fifth-period Heroology classes.

"There are about fifty heroes assigned to first period, plus some troublemaking characters who will try to defeat the heroes," Circe told them. "This means that many of you will need to guide more than one character." Murmurs swept the room. This would be a complicated project!

While everyone watched, Circe pointed her wand at the contents of the trophy cup and began to chant:

"Fly to those you are assigned,

With no hero left behind!"

At her command the tiny scrolls sprouted wings. Lifting the statues they were tethered to out of the trophy cup, they began to flutter around the room like a swarm of determined dragonflies. *Zzzz. Zzzz.* One by one, each found a student to land on.

Athena caught the small statue that dropped into her hands. "I got Argus, the shipbuilder!" she said after reading the small scroll attached to it.

"Seems appropriate. After all, you invented the whole concept of the ship," said Aphrodite.

Athena nodded, heading for the game board. "Argus's scroll says to set him in the city of Iolcus so he can start building a ship right away. I'll design one that's big enough to seat fifty heroes. Sound good, little guy?" Not surprisingly, the statue of Argus didn't reply. Because he was only a wooden game piece. By moving him, though, Athena was causing the real Argus down on Earth to move too.

She set her little Argus in Iolcus, a city on the eastern coast of Greece. It was located almost half-way between Enchantment Academy (which was on an island west of Italy in the Mediterranean Sea) and Medea's dad's kingdom over on the eastern coast of the Black Sea.

"Oh!" said Athena, sounding startled. Right after she'd set Argus on the map, a second statue had dropped into her hand! Medea was close enough to see that it was a wooden boy wearing a lion-skin cape.

"Well, this is weird." Athena glanced around until she spotted a boy standing a few feet away. "I got you as my hero too, Heracles," she told him.

Like the small, carved statue that Athena now held, Heracles also wore a lion-skin cape with great-toothed jaws that fit around his head like a hood. "That's right. I'll be one of the heroes sailing on the real ship with the real Argus," he replied. Grinning, he bowed to her. "And I wouldn't choose anyone else to guide me."

"Aww," said Aphrodite, sighing happily. "That's so sweet." As the goddessgirl of love and beauty, she was always pleased by shows of affection between crushing couples. And it was common knowledge that Athena and Heracles were in *like* with each other!

But that didn't stop Glauce from leaning over to Medea and informing her in a loud voice, "Heracles and Athena are crushes."

Before Medea could tell her she already knew

that, one of the winged scrolls zipped past Glauce's nose, so close that she jerked back. The scroll was headed for Heracles. Instead of being attached to a hero, however, it was bound to a bright golden shield as long as a thumb. He read the scroll aloud: "'Hylas (your shield) will take you to the ship when the time is right.'"

"Why do you get to go on the quest, and not us?" demanded Ares.

"Sometimes it pays to be a mortal like me, god dude. We're the only ones who can be heroes on the game board," Heracles reminded him good-naturedly.

"Does your scroll say anything else, like when the quest is going to begin?" Apollo asked eagerly. Other students leaned in, hoping to find out too.

"Nope," said Heracles. There were mutters of

disappointment, but those changed to excitement as more and more statues delivered themselves to students.

While Medea listened to the chatter around her she also watched Athena, who had found a blank scroll and quill pen and begun to sketch a diagram of a long, narrow ship.

"Hey! I hit the jackpot with my guys," Ares declared, waving a hero in each hand. "I got Polydeuces, the fighter! And Tiphys, the helmsman. He's the ship's pilot!"

"I got royalty—a guy named King Pelias," boasted Poseidon.

"That thing Poseidon's holding is called a trident," Glauce said loudly to Medea.

Medea nodded. She wished Glauce would stop telling her stuff she already knew. Athena and the rest of these MOA students were going to think Medea was uneducated about immortals!

"My scroll says King Pelias is the 'uncle of Jason and usurper of Jason's dad's kingdom in Iolcus.' And I'm supposed to set him in Iolcus immediately too," Poseidon went on. "Who's Jason? And what's a usurper?" he wondered aloud as he took his little statue over to the game board.

Overhearing, Circe replied mysteriously, "Some things you must learn for yourself and others are yet to be revealed."

"A usurper is someone who takes something by force," Athena told Poseidon once he reached her side. Then she gave Circe an apologetic look in case the sorceress might have preferred Poseidon to figure that out on his own.

But Circe only smiled. "Exactly right, Athena.

And just so you all know, it's fine to help or hinder your fellow classmates in this assignment by offering or withholding information."

"Awesome! Only a powerful king could steal a whole kingdom!" said the godboy of the sea. Looking pleased, Poseidon thrust his trident high in the air. Then he set his king statue on the board near Athena's Argus.

Medea watched a scroll fly to a boy with violet-grape-colored eyes. The godboy Dionysus, of course. "Cool! I got some guy named Euphemus. Says here on his scroll that he's got good eyesight. That's bound to be helpful on a quest," said Dionysus.

A scroll flew to Apollo. "Orpheus, the lyre player!" he announced, reading the name of his new hero aloud. "Perfect-o! I can help him work out some cool tunes on the trip!"

"Wow! Orpheus, the dreamy-cute rock star?" Aphrodite said to Athena. Then she pretended to swoon over how cute Orpheus was. Both girls laughed.

Medea and Glauce glanced at each other with excited expressions. Orpheus was a *mega*-famous rock star down on Earth! Naturally, Glauce then had to go and needlessly inform her, "Apollo plays the lyre with Ares and some other godboys in a band called Heavens Above."

"Yeah, I know," Medea informed her back. *Argh!* She wished there were some friendly way to stifle her frenemy's ongoing unnecessary explanations.

"I got two brothers named Zetes and Calais. They've got wings too!" said Pheme, drawing everyone's attention. "Who'd you get?" she asked, peering over Medusa's shoulder. The green girl had just gotten not two but a whole *group* of match-ing characters.

Even from a distance it was easy to know what Pheme said. Her words puffed from her lips in little cloud letters that lingered above her in the air for a few seconds so anyone could read them.

"Wouldn't you like to know?" Medusa teased Pheme gleefully. "I will tell you that they're a bunch of troublemakers. So everybody better watch out!" Without elaborating further, she tucked her small army of statues into the pockets of her chiton.

"Yeah, troublemakers with six arms each!" Pheme crowed, having managed to get a peek at the little statues before Medusa hid them away. The snaky girl just grinned mischievously. Looking intrigued, Pheme tucked Zetes and Calais into her schoolbag. Then she pulled another, larger scroll from the bag and began scribbling something on it with a quill pen.

"Ooh!" said Glauce. "I wonder if Pheme's taking notes on who got which hero and what all's happening. Maybe for her gossip column? I think I'll go over and say hi. Back in a few." With a fluff of her blond hair, Glauce left Medea's side.

Not unhappy to see her go, Medea nodded absently and tuned in to a conversation that had sprung up between Apollo and Medusa. "Sure, Orpheus is a good musician, but what help will that be on a dangerous quest?" the snaky girl was saying to him. "He's not really a strong *physical* hero like Odysseus or Heracles."

"Hate to say it, but she's right, bud," said Ares, causing Apollo to look abashed. "It's not like Orpheus rocking a great tune will save the day if there's a crisis."

"Hey, you never know. I bet all kinds of skills will be needed on this quest," Athena put in, smoothing over the moment.

Apollo brightened. "Yeah, if there's a battle or something, maybe Orpheus could whack enemies over the head with his lyre!" His buds cracked up, laughing heartily.

As more students received heroes—and trouble-making characters, too—one of the flying scrolls suddenly headed for Medea. *Ye gods!* She dodged it, expecting it to continue on and deliver itself to someone else. However, after passing her, it stopped abruptly in midair. Reversing direction, it returned to begin buzzing around her head like a crazed bumble bee. *Buzz-buzz.*

"Go away," she hissed at it. "I'm just a helper here. I'm pretty sure I'm not supposed to get a hero." But did it listen? No! (Maybe because scrolls didn't have ears?)

Glancing around, she realized that no one else had noticed this embarrassing scroll pest. So far, anyway. Trying to escape it before anybody did notice, Medea ducked under the game board table and began to scramble below it on hands and knees from one end to the other. While checking over her shoulder to be sure she wasn't being tailed by that wacko scroll, she saw that the Underworld was on the game board's underside. Interesting! There was Tartarus, the worst place in the Underworld. And the Elysian Fields, the best place. She'd learned about them in both Immortal Studies and *Teen Scrollazine*.

Once she reached the far end of the game board, Medea got to her feet and peered around in relief. Coast clear. *Buzzz.* Or not!

That flying scroll had found her after all! She backed away from it, farther and farther, until she bumped against the back wall of the classroom some distance from the other students. "I'm not the one you want," she told it in a loud whisper, batting at it with her wand. Still it kept circling her. *Help! I'm under attack by a crazed scroll!* she wanted to yell. But she didn't want to draw attention to herself and have others become aware of this totally mortifying situation!

"Hey! I got a bunch of sea nymphs with mermaid tails," the golden-winged Eros announced from across the room. "My scroll says they should some-how cause trouble for the quest. Maybe I should make them fall in love with someone, or something, on board the ship." He shifted the bow and quiver he carried over one shoulder and glanced around at the other students and their statues, as if considering the idea. For some reason his eyes turned thoughtful as they lit on Heracles, Medea noticed.

As the godboy of love, Eros's arrows had a special power. Whoever they pricked fell immediately in love with the very next person they saw. These special arrows were kind of a dangerous gift, in Medea's opinion. If Eros made a mistake, people who didn't like each other one bit could suddenly start crushing!

"Ooh! I got Atalanta!" cooed Aphrodite. "Looks like she'll be in the crew. I wonder if she'll remember me from that race with Hippomenes and the three golden apples. Ever since those two fell in love and got married, they've been living happily ever after!" She sighed with pleasure at the thought.

Meanwhile, Medea had begun trying to flick the

statue that was pursuing her out of the air, but she wasn't having any luck at all!

"Speaking of love," she overheard Eros say to Aphrodite. "Let's work on finishing those new mini arrows we came up with. I just got an idea about how to use them."

"Me too," said Aphrodite. "I was thinking we could shoot some of them to give the ship a fancy send-off!" She and Eros put their heads together then and spoke so quietly that Medea couldn't catch what else they said.

When Medea's attention strayed for a split second, the pesky, crazed flying statue and scroll darted up to hover six inches from her nose. Finally caving, she snatched the carved hero statue in her fist and stared hard at it. She saw at once that it was a teenage boy with chestnut-brown hair and eyes. He wore armor and carried a sword and shield, but for some reason he was only wearing one sandal.

"You're making a mistake," Medea quietly scolded the statue. "I'm just a helper, like I said. So buzz off, okay? Please?" She opened her palm to release the wooden boy, but it didn't budge.

Whoosh! The scroll attached to it unrolled itself. Curious to know the identity of the hero, she lifted him closer and read the info that accompanied him: *Fourteen-year-old Jason, leader of the quest and the son of King Aeson. Set him immediately in the city of Iolcus.*

"*Leader?* No way, mister," she murmured, shaking her finger at the statue. "I cannot, will not, be in charge of the leader of the Hero-ology class quest!" She stepped over to the game board, planning to set the statue on the nearest bit of land.

But before she could accomplish that, Circe

clapped her hands to get everyone's attention. "Who's got Jason?" she called out, her gaze scanning the students. "Speak up, please!"

Medea stopped in her tracks. With the Jason statue clasped in one fist, she whipped her hand behind her back, instinctively wanting to pretend she hadn't gotten the little statue. However, this move accidentally caused its little sword to poke her. She let out a loud, involuntary squeak. "Ow!" All eyes turned her way.

Gulp!

4
Partners

Medea **WENT OVER TO CIRCE AND HELD OUT**
the statue. "Here. This is Jason. Sorry, I think I got
him by mistake."

"Oh, *gnatwings!*" Circe exclaimed, gazing worriedly at her but not taking the statue she'd offered.
"Since you aren't enrolled at MOA, it didn't occur to
me that a scroll might get confused and think you're
participating in the class assignment. You'll have to

keep him now. Once the scrolls choose a student, it's final. Oh, what could it mean, what could it mean?" That faraway, zoned-out expression Circe sometimes got when she was looking inward and searching for answers in her visions came into her eyes.

"Well, I think it means I should've gotten a hero too," Glauce grumped. "How come the scrolls were only confused about Medea?" But Circe was too lost in thought to hear or respond to her.

A zing of gladness zipped through Medea, and she curled her fingers tight around the statue, suddenly *wanting* to keep it. For once she had gotten something Glauce hadn't!

Turning on her heel, she carried her carved Jason statue over to the game board. Pheme followed her, still excitedly jotting notes for her gossip column. Notes about her? Medea wondered. How thrilling!

Everyone else gathered around the board too, but most held on to their heroes for now, since their scrolls hadn't instructed them to do otherwise. Glauce pushed past Pheme till she was right beside Medea. Though Medea held her little hero securely now, she could tell that Glauce was poised to pounce. That girl's hands were opening and closing as if just waiting for the chance to snatch Jason away and set him on the board herself. In other words, Glauce was dying to take charge!

After setting Jason next to King Pelias in the city of Iolcus as the scroll had directed, Medea started thinking. Maybe if she played her cards . . . um . . . *hero* right, this could be her chance to shine in the spotlight.

She imagined herself doing a big display of magic that caused Jason to succeed in whatever his quest was going to be. *Yes!* Despite her rocky beginning here, all was *not* lost. She would watch and wait for the exact right moment to make a big splash and wow everyone this week—including Circe and Glauce! And especially her dad!

"Looks like it's going to be my King Pelias against your Jason," said a boy's voice. While she'd been daydreaming, Poseidon had come over. "So no offense, but I'll be working to sink your hero." (There was the *offense*-ive phrase again!) "And since I'm godboy of the sea and he'll be in a ship, well, he'd better watch out for storms. *Bwah-ha-ha!*"

Medea laughed. "Thanks for the heads-up. Thwarting my hero won't be easy, though. Because I'll be working to keep him afloat," she boasted, having no clue if she really could.

"You do know that Pelias and Jason will make lots

of decisions for themselves, though, right? And some will go against your advice," Medusa remarked. Medea could hear the rapid sound of pen-writing from a little way off. Pheme, taking notes on her conversation with Poseidon and Medusa.

"Guiding the leader of the heroes sounds like it'll be a humongous job. Sure you're up to it?" Glauce asked Medea. "I mean, I'm kind of wondering why Jason is only wearing one sandal. Did you already let him lose his other one?"

"He only had one sandal when I got him," Medea shot back, feeling a bit annoyed at Glauce's question. She hoped it didn't leave some students wondering if she *had* accidentally lost it but was lying. She hadn't! And wasn't! She didn't want these guys to doubt her ability to guide their heroes' leader.

Appearing to have gotten an idea just that

moment, Glauce snapped her fingers, then linked arms with Medea. "I know! Why don't we share the Jason job? It'll be fun. I mean, we are besties, after all!"

Huh? Were they? Glauce had never called her a bestie before. The idea that Glauce thought so highly of her might have filled Medea with happiness before today. But not now, when she was trying to stand out on her own.

Anxious knots formed in Medea's stomach as she tried to think how to reply. Because she knew what "share the Jason job" would really mean. Glauce would take over and take all the credit for whatever work Medea did too! Oh, she'd be all sweet about it, so Medea couldn't point to anything that was unfair about the situation. This kind of thing had happened with Glauce a lot in the past. It was so frustrating, especially because Medea could never explain what this sneaky girl was doing in a way that made sense to anyone else.

Since some other students got more than one hero, maybe you should share with one of them instead, Medea countered silently, trying out the words in her mind. She took a deep breath, planning to repeat those words aloud to her "bestie." However, before she could, Circe swam back out of prophecy-land and into the present.

"Alas!" her aunt announced to the class. "The visions fail me for the moment. We will have to wait to see how all unfolds."

"Medea and I just decided we're going to share Jason!" Glauce informed Circe.

Medea gaped at her, knowing she had certainly *not* given her okay to this plan. Before she could

70

figure a graceful way out of the unwanted partnership, her aunt nodded her agreement.

Then to the whole class Circe said, "Remember, we want Mr. Cyclops to be proud of what we accomplish this week. Those of you with heroes will be graded on your ability to help them get out of whatever trouble they encounter on the way to achieving the goals you set for them. And those of you with troublemakers will be graded on how well they make trouble for the heroes.

"It's your job to decide on your statue's goal or goals, write them on the scrolls that came with your statues, and then drop the scrolls in here." She held up the now-empty trophy cup that had originally contained the statues. "Consider those goals carefully," she went on, setting the trophy down again. "Once written, goals cannot be changed."

"If Jason is the leader of all the heroes, maybe his should be decided first," Athena suggested. "Because it will influence the goals of all the other heroes." Heads turned toward Medea and Glauce.

"Well, um . . ." Medea looked down at the game board and tried to come up with an idea for Jason's goal. However, she was so panicked Glauce would think of something faster than her that her mind went blank. For several horrible seconds she couldn't think of anything at all!

Finally she spoke, working out an idea as she went along. "I guess if Jason's uncle Pelias stole his father's kingdom, then maybe . . ." She paused, unsure, then murmured, "Maybe Jason's goal is to get the kingdom back for—"

"I know! Jason's goal should be to get the king-dom of Iolcus back for his dad!" Glauce shouted.

"Awesome plan!" praised Apollo.

"Thanks," said Glauce. Quickly she took hold of Jason's scroll, wrote down the stated goal, and dropped the scroll into the trophy. Medea just stood there, fuming. Glauce had leapfrogged over her to take credit for her idea! But it would look like sour grapes if she said so.

"Not so fast," Poseidon challenged, crossing his arms over his chest. "King Pelias isn't going to hand that kingdom back just because Jason asks him to."

"Excellent!" Circe told him. "Mr. Cyclops would be pleased that you're already thinking of roadblocks for the heroes, to test their mettle."

Hmph! thought Medea, not one bit pleased by Poseidon's challenge. Though if quests were easy, she supposed, they wouldn't be quests!

"It's magnificent! Just like I pictured," said a

delighted voice. The students looked over to see Athena examining a small ship model that had appeared on the game board off the coast of Iolcus. The ship was long and narrow, with a raised platform at the front and back, and twenty-five benches set along either side for a total of fifty. There was a big, square white sail lashed to its central masthead.

"How'd you do that?" Medea asked Athena. "Make the ship show up on the board? Is there a big one like it in actual Iolcus now too?"

Without looking up from her study of the ship, the goddessgirl smiled and nodded. "Yes. See, if an immortal sketches ideas on papyrus but doesn't bespell them to stay put there, gravity will cause them to fall off the page as actual objects," she explained. "I learned that the hard way my first week at MOA when I brainstormed a bunch of inventions that accidentally rained down on the heads of mortals on Earth!"

Poseidon read aloud the name painted on the model ship's side. "*Argo*."

"In honor of Argus, the shipbuilder?" guessed Pheme.

"So is the real ship down on Earth ready for its crew?" asked Apollo at the same time.

When Athena nodded yes to both questions, students began setting their heroes in place on the benches on board the ship. That must be why these statues were smaller than Odysseus and the other old ones had been, Medea decided. So they'd all fit aboard this one little model ship!

Aphrodite looked over from the mini arrows she and Eros were working on, to critically eye the unpainted wooden armor, swords, and spears carved on the hero statues. "Their armor is pretty drab," she noted. "And bronze is trending this season." (Trending because of Aphrodite, according to last week's *Teen Scrollazine*, Medea knew.)

Momentarily abandoning her arrow project, the fashion-forward goddessgirl fetched jars of paint from the supply closet. Then, with the help of a half dozen students, the heroes were lifted one by one to have their armor, shields, and weapons painted metallic bronze with red trim. Only Jason would be painted differently, it was decided—in silver and red—so he'd stand out as the leader.

"Ye gods! That gear looks mega-amazing," Athena commented as she watched the students work. "I just thought of something to spiff up the ship, too!" So saying, she pulled the polished wooden stick out of her updo twist, causing her hair to drift down past her shoulders in soft waves. Now it looked the way she usually wore it in drawings Medea had seen of her.

After a quick trip to the supply closet, Athena was back, hammering tiny wooden pegs into the polished hair stick to attach it to the prow (the front end of the ship). The top end of the stick was carved with the head and torso of a woman with long, flowing hair, Medea saw now.

Noticing the curious gazes around her, Athena explained, "I thought this would look cool as a nautical figurehead. Plus, it's magic—carved from the wood of a sacred tree that grows in the forest of an oracle named Dodona. Any part of that magical tree can speak, which means this figurehead will be able to act as lookout for the crew and warn them of any dangers looming ahead of the ship."

"Before they set sail, can we give the crew a catchy name that'll sound good in my column?" Pheme suggested, tapping her pen on her chin in thought. "I know! How about the Argoquesters?" When no one seemed to like that nickname, she tried others. "The Argoadventurers? Argotroopers? Argonauts?" Many in the class sounded their approval for her last nickname, so she wrote it down in her notes.

Circe had been watching and listening to the students' progress, and now she spoke up. "There's not much time left in class today. Please complete any painting in the next few minutes and set all the statues on the ship. Those of you with troublemaker statues, finish deciding their goals and then place them anywhere you choose on the map."

Excitement rippled throughout the classroom now that the quest was close to getting under way.

"Wait! There's something you guys should know," Poseidon announced. As soon as he had everyone's attention, he pointed to the two statues on Iolcus. "Down on Earth, my King Pelias and Jason have been talking. And Pelias has agreed to give Jason's dad back his throne." He paused dramatically, then added, "On one condition."

Pheme licked her orange-glossed lips in anticipation. "What condition?" she asked, her pen hovering over her notescroll.

"Jason must steal the famous Golden Fleece!" Poseidon declared. "Only then will King Pelias return the kingdom of Iolcus to Jason's dad."

Medea's shocked gasp was drowned out when students immediately buzzed with questions. "Fleece? The one Pheme wrote about in *Teen Scrollazine* a few weeks ago?" "The one in Colchis?" "Doesn't a king named Aeëtes have a dragon guarding that thing?"

Poseidon nodded yes to all, then started laughing his joking-evil laugh again. *"Bwah-ha-ha!"* Quickly he wrote something on the scroll that had come with his king statue and dropped it in the trophy. His king's goal!

"I bet Pelias is expecting Jason to fail, so he'll get to keep Iolcus for himself!" Pheme guessed.

Poseidon grinned. "My lips are sealed."

"Ha! Our heroes pitted against a dragon? Bring it on!" cheered Apollo.

"What an awesome battle that will be!" hurrahed Ares.

"Yeah, with the dragon winning!" said Poseidon.

"You wish!" said Athena.

Of course, all of this was no joking matter to Medea. Or to Circe, either, who paled and pulled her aside. "Oh dear! I must tell you something," her aunt began, speaking softly so no one else would hear. "Two days ago I had a vision that a thief would steal the fleece. I've just realized that thief will likely be Jason! There's nothing I can do to stop him now that Poseidon has set his goal, so I can only do my best to protect you."

Having eavesdropped on her aunt and dad talking, Medea had already guessed this about Jason the minute Poseidon mentioned the fleece. Thing was, Medea was kind of jealous of that fleece. *Would it be so bad if it got stolen?* she wondered for about half a second. *Yes!* she decided, because her dad would be really upset!

Hearing laughter over by the game board, Medea glanced toward it. Poseidon was joking around, coaxing sea monsters to jump through a hoop to entertain the students who were painting the last of the Argonaut statues. And Glauce was busy nearby, buddying up to Pheme again.

Circe went on, pulling Medea's attention. "So anyway, I'm not sure it's a good idea for you to guide this quest after all."

"What? Yes it is!" Medea protested. "*Poseidon* made it Jason's goal to get the fleece, not me. That means I can still try to stop Jason." Stop him from supposedly stealing her heart, too! Her aunt hadn't mentioned that part of the prophecy, so she didn't either, since doing so would reveal she'd eavesdropped yesterday.

Circe shook her head. "Too risky. There's more you don't know. Evidently, when the thief steals the fleece, it is foretold that he will also steal your heart and dethrone your father! No, you and Glauce will be safest far away from Jason, back at Enchantment Academy. And that's final."

Medea's eyes bugged out as she focused on one part of what her aunt had just said. "Dethrone? You mean as in steal our kingdom?" she asked. Circe nodded.

Medea stood there, stunned. Why had her dad and her aunt failed to mention this plot to dethrone her dad to her? But she knew the answer. Probably her dad thought he was protecting her somehow by keeping the information secret!

Circe waved Glauce over and then touched the tip of her wand to both of the girls' wands in turn. "There. I've set your wands to send you both back to Enchantment Academy, five minutes after the *Argo* launches. Medea, since you don't have a room in the dorm, you'll stay in my apartment during my absence for the rest of the week and go to classes there as usual. I'll accompany you to Colchis to explain everything to your dad upon my return to the academy at the weekend."

"Huh? You're sending us back to EA before the quest even starts? Why?" asked Glauce. She glared at Medea. "Okay, what did you do to ruin everything this time?"

"Nothing!" exclaimed Medea.

"It's not Medea's fault. I have my reasons," Circe told her. "You girls can watch the launch here in class, but afterward your wands will whisk you away. I'll simply explain to these MOA students that you were called home."

Glumly, Medea and Glauce trudged back to the game board. Wasn't there any way she could fix things? Medea wondered in desperation. Maybe she should snatch the little Jason statue from the game board and throw him out the classroom window. No, someone would surely retrieve him and the quest would continue. Everyone's goals had been committed to paper and put in the trophy by now, and so could not be undone.

"Gather around, everyone, and we'll launch the *Argo*," Circe proclaimed. "Once it sets sail, the quest will officially begin!" This announcement was greeted with class-wide cheers.

Her mind racing, Medea watched Athena guide the ship into the Aegean Sea, which was a section of the Mediterranean Sea east of Greece. With Glauce on her right and Heracles to her left, Medea looked around the circle of MOA students gathered at the game board. Athena and Aphrodite had been especially nice to her, and she didn't really want to be a rat and ruin their chances of completing this quest. Their grades would suffer. Not only that—mortals everywhere would hear about their failure and possibly think less of them.

Still, she had to find a way to protect her dad! *Think! Think! There must be some way to sabotage this mission and save my family's kingdom!* Her aunt might believe there was no way to change a prophecy, but it was worth a try!

"Aren't you supposed to be on that ship?" Dionysus called to Heracles from across the table.

Pushing his lion cape over his shoulders, Heracles gestured to the tiny square shield he held between two fingers. "Yeah, Hylas here is supposed to take me aboard the *Argo* when the time is right. I hope that's soon, so I don't hold things up."

Just then a volley of mini arrows trailing

bronze, silver, and red streamers sailed over the game table. The other kids craned their necks to see that, with Aphrodite's help, Eros had fired off the celebration arrows from across the room. No one except Medea noticed when one of them pricked Heracles' forearm, leaving a small pink heart-shaped mark before it fell to the edge of the game board between him and her. She carefully picked up the arrow before it could fall to the floor and stab her foot.

Meanwhile, Eros and Aphrodite shouted, "Three cheers for our new quest!"

"Woo-hoo! Hooray!" the students called out in return.

"You okay?" Medea asked the muscular mortal boy beside her. But Heracles was too busy staring at his shield with a weird, besotted expression to reply.

The students cheered a second time. "Woot! Woot!"

Eros and Aphrodite were eyeing Heracles and whispering now. Hey! thought Medea. If you were struck by one of Eros's mini arrows, you'd crush on the very first person you saw afterward. Did that apply to the first *thing* you saw as well? When that arrow struck Heracles, he had been looking at Hylas. Was he now crushing on that shield? And had Eros purposely aimed that arrow to cause trouble for one of the *Argo*'s heroes already? Namely, Heracles himself?

"Yay! Hooray!" the students cheered a third and final time. Everyone began calling out encouragements to their heroes or troublemakers. "Bon voyage!" "Good luck!" "Go, Argonauts!"

Noticing that the ship was moving farther out to sea, Medea panicked. Without thinking, she shoved the little arrow into the pocket of her chiton instead of returning it to Eros as she'd halfway meant to do. All she cared about right now was convincing her aunt to let her stay before it was too late! As she turned from the game board to go to her, Medea's hand bumped Heracles', causing him to drop his small shield and her to drop her wand. Both objects fell into the game board sea! *Plop! Plop!*

"No! Hylas!"

"No! My wand!"

Heracles and Medea reached out at the same time to save them from sinking. Medea rescued her wand with her right hand. Then she made a grab with her left to help Heracles. And for a moment . . . both of them held the shield in their fingers.

She drew a quick, surprised breath and heard him do the same. A dizzy, tingly feeling was enveloping her. And the classroom looked strangely fuzzy, like it was fading away around her. In the excitement, no one else in the classroom seemed to notice something odd was happening. Except Glauce. She clasped Medea by the elbow, giving her arm a hard shake. "You okay?" she asked.

"Whah?" Medea replied woozily. Was this Circe's travel magic she was experiencing? No, this magic felt different somehow. Why did the other students look so far away and hazy all of a sudden, when Glauce and Heracles did not? Maybe because she, Heracles, and Glauce were connected by touch?

"Good-bye, Medea! Glauce! I'll see you girls back at Enchantment Academy on Saturday," Medea heard her aunt call out. And then abruptly the world around Medea morphed into blue sea and sky.

Splash!

5

The Argo

*G*LUB, GLUB. MEDEA WAS ALONE, SOPPING WET
and treading water.

"Where am I?" she wondered aloud. Still clenching her wand in one fist, she fought the cold waves
that were seesawing her high and then low. She'd
made a splash, all right, but not the fabulous kind
she'd dreamed of making to impress everyone at
MOA. She was in the sea!

Hearing the creak of timber, the rumble of voices, and the sound of beautiful lyre music, she whirled around in the water. Then she gasped. There was a huge wooden ship alongside her! It was long and narrow, with the name *Argo* painted on its side.

Splash! In the very next second Glauce dropped into the sea beside her, then came up sputtering. "Hey! Are we where I think we are? Smack in the middle of the Hero-ology quest? No offense, but you've really messed up this time!" she snapped at Medea. "And your wand's in fifth position, by the way. I'd change to first, since it looks like we'll be traveling." Glauce hooked a thumb toward the ship.

Fifth position had Medea pinching her wand between the tips of her index finger and thumb. It was the way the EA band director held her baton while conducting a musical performance, and also used for doing quick, precisely directed magic. Some people accidentally dropped their wands in this position, but Medea never had. She liked fifth!

Ignoring the wand position suggestion, she concentrated on figuring out their situation. "The last thing I remember from class is trying to help Heracles keep Hylas from sinking, and you asking me if I was okay. That little shield's magic must've transported all three of us here!"

Glauce nodded. "But where's Heracles?"

"Intruder alert! Intruder alert!"

Both girls glanced up at the ship in surprise. The carved figurehead on its prow had spotted them and was sounding an alarm. It was the figurehead Athena had made from the polished stick in her hair updo, only now it was way bigger and curved tightly along the full-size ship's prow. Unfortunately, Athena had been right that it would be able to speak. In fact, it was kind of being a blabbermouth!

Before the girls could think what to do, a net fell over them and they were hoisted onto the *Argo*.

Thunk! The net hit the ship's deck and both girls rolled out of it. Medea sat up, combing seaweed out of her hair and looking around.

Just like Athena's little ship model on the MOA game board, this ship had one huge, square white mainsail at its center, a raised platform at either end, and benches on both sides. One hero sat on each bench, clutching an oar. But the fifty or so crew members had all stopped rowing to stare suspiciously at the two girls.

"Spies!" "King Pelias must've sent 'em!" the sailors roared.

Medea and Glauce scrambled to their feet, totally

soaked and dripping water. "We're not working with King Pelias," Medea protested as the girls did their best to wring out the hems of their chitons. However, she *was* a spy! A spy who had just now decided she might be able to use this unexpected opportunity to somehow stop Jason from stealing her dad's Golden Fleece!

"Then what are you doing here?" asked a new voice. Both girls swung around to behold the boy who'd spoken. He had brown hair and eyes, and wore only one sandal. And he was the only member of the crew wearing silver armor with red trim instead of bronze.

"Jason?" both girls asked.

His eyes narrowed at this, and he planted his fists at his hips. "Only spies would know my name."

He looked like his carved statue stand-in, only

cuter, Medea thought grudgingly. Still, she did not feel the slightest bit of a crush on him. So if the part of the prophecy about him stealing her heart was wrong, her fingers were crossed that the part about him stealing the fleece would turn out to be wrong too!

"We know you're Jason because we're helping the gods and goddesses of Mount Olympus to make sure you get the fleece," Glauce chimed in. She might think this was true, but it wasn't Medea's plan. Not at all!

Jason's eyebrows lowered and he took a menacing step toward them. "How do you know what we Argonauts seek?" he demanded fiercely.

"Spies! Walk the plank!" yelled Athena's Dodona figurehead. Other crew members took up this call, chanting her words.

"No! Wait! Oh, there's Heracles. He knows us," said Medea, waving. "Yoo-hoo, Heracles, remember us?"

Like they'd suspected, he had been magicked here at the same time as them, but he must have landed on board instead of in the water. He was already sitting on one of the benches near the prow, Hylas at his side. During transport, that shield had somehow magically enlarged to the exact right size for him to use in battle.

"Is she telling the truth?" Jason asked the muscular, lion-skin-caped boy.

"Dunno," Heracles answered, shrugging disinterestedly. He was gazing at his shield with an adoring look on his face—the same look he'd given it in the classroom after being struck by Eros's arrow.

Medea looked around for someone else who might

help them. Her gaze landed on a guy standing at the stern (the back part of the ship). He was holding on to a horizontal bar of wood called a tiller, which was connected to the rudder under the boat and used as a lever for steering. This had to be one of Ares' heroes, Tiphys, the ship's pilot. He looked as suspicious of her and Glauce as most of the crew, however. No help would come from him, she thought.

Her gaze moved on. Over on the fifth bench up from the tiller portside Medea finally saw a friendly face. Right away she knew from drawings she'd seen of her in *Teen Scrollazine* that this Argonaut had to be Atalanta. She looked strong and athletic, and had hair almost as long and golden as that of the goddess-girl who would guide her on this quest—Aphrodite. Atalanta was smiling at Medea and Glauce as if not at all worried they were spies. Yay! Sisterhood!

"Don't make us walk the plank. We can help you. We have magic wands," Glauce announced, waving hers around.

"Magic wands! Magic wands!" squawked the figurehead.

Hearing her, the whole crew grew tenser still. "Hand 'em over," demanded Jason, holding out his palm.

"Sure. Here you go," said Glauce. In a flash she'd snatched away Medea's wand and given both of their wands to Jason.

To Medea's surprise, he immediately threw them overboard! *Plunk! Plunk!*

Medea ran to the rail in time to watch the two wands sink. She rounded on Glauce in frustration. "Why did you give them to him?" She felt totally unprotected without her wand!

"He's the boss. But, well, I didn't expect him to do *that*!" said Glauce, gesturing to where he'd tossed them.

"Count yourselves lucky I don't throw you both to the sea monsters too!" declared Jason.

"Sea monsters?" echoed Glauce. She and Medea exchanged worried glances. Medea hadn't been concerned about Medusa's snakes or the cute little sea monsters on the game board. But real sea monsters were something else. Something scary. No way did she want to become a sea monster snack!

Just then a winged messagescroll swooped down from the clear blue sky to land on Jason's shoulder. As he read the scroll, his eyes widened. "Listen to this, guys!" he called out to his crew in an excited voice.

"And *girls*!" Atalanta yelled. She, Medea, and

Glauce were the only three girls on the *Argo* (if you didn't count the figurehead). Atalanta was by far the oldest of the three, however. Maybe as old as twenty!

"Oh yeah. Sorry, Atalanta," said Jason, shooting her a grin. "So anyway, this messagescroll is from that famous poet, Apollonius. He says he heard about our quest and wants to try something new. He wants to write a musical about it, if our exploits prove entertaining enough!"

Jason glanced at a boy seated near the middle of the ship on a starboard bench. Many of the heroes had weapons, like bows and arrows or spears, at their sides. But this boy had a lyre. And he was just as dreamy-cute as Aphrodite had described him back at MOA.

"Orpheus! Apollonius wants us to keep a record

of what happens," Jason called to him. "Names, places, adventures. I think you're the perfect crew member for the task."

"Awesome!" said Orpheus, punching a fist high in the air. "And since he wants to make our story into a musical, I'll put all that info into *songs* about our adventures. Once I sing a tune, I never forget it, so I won't have to bother with pen and papyrus till later."

"Excellent!" said Jason. "At the end of our voyage we'll send your work to Apollonius. Just think! If he does turn your songs into a musical show, everyone will want to go see it at the Theatre of Dionysus. Our quest will be celebrated by all for many years to come!"

The crew cheered.

"Yeah, so everybody, please try to do interesting

stuff worthy of celebration from now on so I can write good, catchy songs, okay?" Orpheus advised.

Medea sensed the heightened enthusiasm of the crew. The news of Apollonius's interest in their quest seemed to have made them more determined than ever to excel at it. Which didn't help her one bit! Thanks a lot, Apollonius!

Glauce had gone uncharacteristically silent and was now staring at Jason with a weird look on her face. What was she thinking about? From her soft smile you might guess her thoughts were of something really happy. Like birthday presents or getting into the Magicasters Club at school. Which made no sense, because their lives were in serious peril right now!

Abruptly a breeze blew up, rocking the ship. While the crew got back to rowing, Medea and Glauce ran over and grabbed hold of the central masthead to steady themselves. Jason seemed to forget them for the moment as he shouted new orders to his crew to secure the *Argo*'s safety.

"I wonder why Circe hasn't magicked us out of here yet," Medea said to Glauce over the rising wind.

"Duh! Because she thinks she magicked us to Enchantment Academy. Weren't you listening when she called bye and said she'd see us on Saturday?" Glauce replied. "Maybe not, since you were busy messing up her plan by getting mixed up with Heracles' shield." She paused to glance over at Jason again with that weird look in her eyes. It was the same way Heracles was looking at Hylas, the shield. "Not that I'm complaining," she added softly.

Medea thought about how the shield had accidentally transported them here along with Heracles.

"Hmm," she said, "do you think the kids back in Hero-ology can see us as statues on the game board?" Before Glauce could respond, she answered her own question. "Oh, wait. Only the statues from Mr. Cyclops's trophy cup are officially part of the game, so I bet no one sees us here. And if that's true, then—"

"Then no one will come looking for us until the end of the week, when Circe goes back to EA and finds out we aren't there," finished Glauce. Leaning back against the mast, she watched Jason running around giving orders, and sighed happily. "Which is fine by me."

"Did one of Eros's arrows get you, by any chance?" Medea asked her carefully.

"Nuh-uh, why do you ask?"

Medea spread her hands, palms up, to indicate,

106

Isn't it obvious? When Glauce just gave her a puzzled look, she added, "Because you gave Jason our wands? And you're looking at him . . . funny?"

Glauce wrinkled her nose. "Funny? I don't know what you mean."

"Land ho!" a crewman yelled, drawing their attention. He was directly above them, high in the crow's nest atop the ship's mast.

The figurehead rolled her eyes. "That's such a boring announcement. And it doesn't tell the whole story. You should've said: 'Bunch of boy-crazy girls dead ahead on the beach!'"

At this intriguing information, all eyes turned in the direction of the island they were fast approaching in the Aegean Sea. "Look at all those girls jumping up and down, Zetes!" exclaimed one of the rowing sailors.

The sailor on the seat across the aisle from him replied, "Yeah, there must be a hundred of them! And they're waving us over."

Both boys had red hair and freckles, and wings growing from their backs, Medea saw. These had to be Pheme's heroes, the brothers Zetes and Calais!

"I say we keep going," Glauce piped up. "For all we know, those girls might be planning to throw spears at us as soon as we get closer. It's not worth taking a chance."

"But you can't just make a beeline for Colchis," Medea reasoned to Jason. "Stopping on this island is just the kind of interesting adventure you need to spice up that musical Apollonius wants to do about your quest." Her real reason for suggesting a stop was that it would also slow the quest down and give her more time to think about how she could prevent

Jason from stealing her dad's Golden Fleece!

Many crew members nodded their heads in agreement, but Glauce glared at her.

"Right! We're stopping. Everybody off!" called Jason. He motioned to Medea and Glauce, saying, "And that includes you two."

Turning toward two of the crew, Jason amended his order. "But not you guys. Tiphys, while we're gone, I'll trust you to plan our navigation from here. And Heracles, you'll stay on board to stand guard."

The minute the rest of the Argonauts disembarked, dozens of girls wearing chitons woven from sea grass ran up to them. They didn't throw spears. But they did throw compliments.

"Ooh! Cute guy alert!" said one, giggling. They were only interested in the boys and pretty much ignored Medea, Glauce, and Atalanta.

"Gosh! You all look so strong!" said another, clapping her hands at the sight of the boys as if they were cookies on a plate. Flattered, some of the crew members began posing in ways that showed off their muscles. This display was greeted with great approval by the silly girls.

Then the sailors' crowd of admirers parted to make a path for a girl wearing a very fancy sea-grass chiton and a tall crown made of grapes, cherries, and apricots. She walked right up to Jason. Batting her eyelashes at him, she said, "Welcome to Lemnos, the eighth-largest island in Greece! I am Hypsipyle. And you are Jason?"

He looked at her in surprise. "How did you know?"

"Pheme, of course!" trilled Hypsipyle. "She is spreading the word all over Earth about the musical

Apollonius plans to create about your exploits. And now that you've chosen Lemnos to be the first stop on your quest, we'll be famous! Our economy will skyrocket and we'll get lots more tourists coming here. Mostly boys, we hope!"

Before Jason could reply, Hypsipyle summoned an artist to draw a sketch of the two of them. "And speaking of boys, wowee-wow-wow! You are super *kee-YUTE*!" she told Jason as the artist worked. "And talk about a strongman! I bet you could lift the *Argo* above your head with no trouble at all! And maybe even spin it around on the tip of your finger!"

"Well, uh, I . . ." Jason seemed unsure how to respond to this over-the-top praise.

Once the artist had finished her drawing, Hypsipyle instructed her to send it off to Pheme right away. "You must hang out for a while," she told Jason and his crew. "Anybody hungry? We'll make lunch."

"Good idea. And we'd love to get a tour of your island!" enthused Medea. The longer she could delay the *Argo*, the better. She racked her brain for a way to thwart Jason's quest. Would one of these girls agree to get a warning to her dad about Jason's plan to steal the fleece? More likely they'd rat her out to Jason, since they adored him.

With Medea's encouragement, the Lemnos girls proceeded to show the crew every corner of their island, from its lovely sandy beaches to its picturesque (but smelly) sheep pastures. Then they all enjoyed a lunch on the beach, dining on figs, melons, olives, cheeses, and meats.

Unfortunately, Glauce was working at cross-purposes to Medea. "We're wasting time!" she kept telling Jason. "The sooner you finish your quest, the sooner you'll become famous heroes."

After hours of listening to her constant grumbling about how they needed to get going, the crew began to get antsy too. They began to say things like: "She's right." "Makes sense." "Let's get a move on!"

Eventually Jason agreed that they should go.

It took a while to convince the super-friendly Lemnos girls to let them leave, however. When they finally did, Hypsipyle gave Jason a new pair of sandals and a frilly, dove-shaped pillow with JASON LOVES LEMNOS! embroidered on it.

"Thanks," said Jason, appearing pleased. "I can use the pillow as a bench cushion!"

"Just a sample of the souvenirs we're going to be

marketing to tourists!" she informed him. "We're also making Jason action figures and toy Argonaut helmets."

As the heroes began climbing aboard the ship again, the Lemnos girls tossed each of them a souvenir pillow shaped like one of the birds of their island. At last Jason and his crew took their oars in hand, sighing with happiness as they sat on the cushy pillows they'd set beneath themselves on their benches.

Medea and Glauce hadn't been given pillows, but they found comfortable-enough perches on the two large coils of rope that naturally formed chairlike bowls, located halfway between the stern and the main mast. Luckily, their chitons, sandals, and hair had dried by now.

"This pillow is so comfy," Medea heard Jason comment as the ship slid through the water. "It was really nice of Hypsipyle to give it to me. And this new pair of sandals, too, since I was missing one."

Hypsipyle might be nice, but she was also smart when it came to business dealings. Medea had a feeling that girl planned to use the single sandal Jason had left behind on Lemnos as a tourist attraction!

The more Jason talked about Hypsipyle, the sourer Glauce's expression got. Seeing how unhappy she looked, Medea felt kind of sorry for her. Normally, her frenemy wasn't the type to crush any more than *she* was, but Medea was pretty sure Glauce was crushing now—on Jason!

On the heels of this thought an idea bloomed in Medea's brain. Carefully she reached into her pocket. Luckily, that mini arrow of Eros's was still there. *Hmm.* What if she could somehow manage to prick Jason with it while he happened to be looking at Glauce? It would cause him to crush on her, which would make Glauce happy. Then, once Jason was crushing on her, Glauce might be able to talk him into giving up on his quest to steal the fleece. But for this plan to succeed, Medea would first need to convince *Glauce* that this quest was a terrible idea.

So, stretching her arms and giving a big fake yawn, Medea said casually, "Who knows how many more islands of cute girls there are between us and Colchis? I bet Jason and this crew are going to have tons of girlfriends and souvenirs by the time we get there and this quest ends."

"Huh?" Glauce looked alarmed.

"Oh, sorry, do you . . . do you *like* him? I mean *like*-like him?" Medea asked, trying to look surprised by this notion. "In that case, maybe we should try to cut this whole quest thing short. That way he won't meet any more girls. And he won't steal from my dad, either. It's a win-win." Unfortunately, Glauce looked unconvinced as well as not quite ready to admit her crush. Had Medea pushed too hard too soon?

Just then Orpheus began singing a little song he'd made up after the crew's adventure on Lemnos:

> *"Hypsipyle gave Jason a soft pillow dove.*
> *Could this mean that those two are falling in love?"*

Jason's cheeks reddened. "What? No!"

Glauce gritted her teeth in irritation. "'Love,' my foot!" she muttered. Leaning toward Medea, she murmured, "You know, maybe you're right about cutting this quest short. We'll just have to figure out how."

"I might know a way," Medea told her mysteriously.

"You'd better let me in on the plan, whatever it is," Glauce insisted. "We don't want to take a chance of you messing up again."

Grr. Gritting her teeth, Medea ignored the remark.

6

Troublemakers

THE NEXT MORNING MEDEA STOOD AT THE RAIL
of the *Argo*, her chiton and her long black hair whipping in the stiff sea breeze. She and Glauce had slept
curled up on the rope coils, which had been made
more comfortable by the loan of Zetes's and Calais's
pillows. Those boys and the rest of the crew had slept
on their benches throughout the night, except when
taking turns as lookouts and oarsmen.

Though Jason's bench was dead center at the very back of the ship near the tiller so he could see straight up the main aisle and keep an eye on everything and everyone, he was rarely seated there, Medea noticed. Instead he was usually among the crew, talking over problems or offering instructions as the ship started through a long, narrow passage called the Dardanelles that would take them from the Aegean Sea into the smaller Sea of Marmara.

She patted the pocket of her chiton, feeling the shape of Eros's magic arrow inside it. By now the *Argo* had been at sea for a day and a night. But while the whole crew was around, she hadn't dared to put her plan into action. The last thing she needed was for Jason to get pricked by the arrow, then start crushing on an Argonaut he spotted instead of Glauce!

As if the crewman high in the crow's nest had

heard her thoughts and wanted to help get the crew off the boat (which seemed unlikely), he suddenly shouted, "Land ahoy!"

"Yeah, I think we can all see that," the figurehead called back to him. "Could you puh-*leeze* try to put a little more excitement into your announcements? Something like: 'Towering, mysterious mountain looming dead ahead! Beware!'"

A very tall mountain was indeed sticking up from a spit of land about a half mile ahead of the ship near the entrance from the Aegean Sea to the Sea of Marmara, Medea saw. But whether or not that was cause for concern was yet to be seen.

"Take us in, Tiphys!" ordered Jason. "We'll dock and climb that peak. I've got a bad feeling about what lies beyond it, so it can't hurt to check."

Heracles nodded. "Good idea. You never know.

There could be pirates or sea monsters waiting to attack us in the channels on either side of the mountain, where it's too narrow for us to turn around and escape."

Much to Medea's disappointment, after the ship was docked, Jason instructed Tiphys, Heracles, Glauce, and her to stay on board the *Argo*. Only he and the rest of the Argonauts would hike up the mountain. That wasn't going to help her get him and Glauce paired off. She needed him to stay on board with them!

If she had thought it would do any good, Medea might've protested, but Jason seemed pretty headstrong. Push him or his crew too far and she might find herself tossed overboard as sea monster food!

She and Glauce sat gloomily on a vacant bench near the gangway as the sailors filed off the ship.

Medea perked up when she realized that Jason, who was at the end of the line, would be the last person to pass by Glauce and her. Finally! The time to put her arrow-pricking plan into action had come!

She nudged her shoulder against Glauce's as Jason approached. "You should stand up and wish him good luck before he heads out."

"Great idea," said Glauce, looking at her in surprise. "Once in a while you do have one."

Medea arched an eyebrow. *Only once in a while?* That was a backhanded compliment if ever she'd heard one. Typical Glauce!

The Jason-crushing girl smoothed her blond hair and sat up straighter, poised to rise from the bench when he reached them. Meanwhile, Medea bent and pretended to adjust her sandal straps with one hand, while reaching into her pocket with her other.

From the corner of her eye she observed Jason moving closer . . . and closer. Her fingers gripped the mini arrow, preparing to pull it out and lightly prick his leg with its tip.

Suddenly footsteps echoed from somewhere up the mountainside. *Stomp! Stomp! Stomp!*

"Look *owwwt!* A horde of giants is coming our way!" Atalanta called back to shore. The fastest runner (and hiker!) among them, she'd taken the lead up the mountain while most of the Argonauts were still onshore. Above her a dozen or so giants had rounded over the mountaintop and were now marching in formation down toward the *Argo.*

Lickety-split, Jason raced past Glauce and Medea and leaped from the ship to join his crew and confront the giants. *Drat!* Medea had missed her chance!

The giants chanted a terrifying tune in time to their marching as they readied an attack on the Argonauts.

>*"We are the Earthbound Men.*
>
>*We have six arms built in.*
>
>*We'll stomp your ship, then grin.*
>
>*We always like to win.*
>
>*We are the Earthbound Men."*

"That's a terrible—not to mention *mean*—song," Orpheus yelled to the giants from where he stood onshore. Hearing this, the biggest and scariest of the Earthbound Men gave a roar and headed straight for him. Orpheus paled, hugged his lyre, and ran. Even if he had known of Apollo's idea to use his lyre to whack an enemy in battle, if he'd tried it these giants would probably have flicked him away like a bug!

As Jason surged ahead of him to confront the giant, Orpheus turned to watch. Walking hastily backward toward the ship now, he strummed his lyre and sang:

> *"That E-Man looks scary,*
>
> *Not like a good friend.*
>
> *Jason, say bye-bye,*
>
> *This looks like the end."*

Jason glared at Orpheus over his shoulder. "Not helping!"

"Sorry!" Orpheus told him. "But I think Apollonius would want me to call situations like I see 'em."

The E-Men, as Orpheus had nicknamed them,

really did have six arms "built in." Two grew from their shoulders and four jutted from their sides. And they did indeed look super-scary just like in his song!

"Those must be Medusa's troublemakers!" Medea exclaimed to Glauce. "Remember? She got a whole group of matching statues in class that each had six arms. Isn't it great? Her E-Men are delaying the *Argo*!"

"No! It is *not* great at all," said Glauce, pointing at the giants, who were getting closer. "Medusa seems to be sending those giants to stomp the ship. And guess what we're standing on!"

The girls stared at each other with big eyes. *Arghhh!* They both ran for the gangway, but Heracles was blocking their exit. He'd grabbed the nearest bow and quiver of arrows and now stood eyeing the oncoming giants.

"Back off, you dumb ol' E-Men!" he hollered. He pulled his bowstring and shot off an arrow. It soared in a high arc, then zoomed downward to stick in the biggest giant's big toe.

"Owie-ow-ow!" yelled the giant. Hopping around on one foot, he pointed at Heracles. "Waaah! Meanie! You shot my piggy toe!" (He was so enormous that his big toe was the size of an actual pig!) Seeing what had happened, the other giants turned into whimpering wimps, too. They beat a hasty retreat up and over the mountaintop, shouting insults at Heracles the whole time. "Bully! Toe-shooter! Ruffian!"

They didn't even pause when they stomped upward past Atalanta, who was heading down to the ship. She'd circled around the giants while they were marching to the shore and had continued to the top of the mountain to see what was on its other side.

"All looks clear ahead!" Medea heard her shout to Jason.

"Onward, Argonauts!" Jason ordered when they were all back aboard the ship. "Tiphys, set sail!"

"Good aim with that arrow," he commended Heracles, who looked pleased by the praise.

Strumming his lyre as they pulled up anchor, Orpheus quickly composed another song:

"Those E-Men were chickens who ran away fast.
Now we can continue our journey at last."

It was kind of short, thought Medea. But Orpheus was probably in a hurry because a new blustery storm was blowing in! Within minutes enormous waves brought the ship low, then lifted it high, turning them every which way in the process.

"Poseidon at work back at MOA, I bet!" Medea yelled to Glauce as they clung to the tall central mast to keep from being swept out to the sea. "He promised to make stormy trouble for Jason, remember?"

"Yeah, I can just picture him leaning over the Hero-ology game board, laughing that evil 'bwah-ha-ha' laugh of his and blowing at the *Argo* as hard as he can," said Glauce. "I wonder if he'd let up a little if he knew we were on this ship. His storm's making me kind of seasick!"

"Doubt it," Medea yelled back. "He wants to make a good Hero-ology grade!" What that godboy of the sea also didn't know was that she was on *his* side now. Despite the rocking and rolling of the ship, she was actually glad for the delay Poseidon was causing.

Any action that slowed Jason from getting the fleece was A-OK with her!

"Can our ship withstand these gusts, Argus?" Jason hollered to a young man with dark, curly hair cropped close to his head.

Hearing him call the familiar name of Athena's shipbuilder, Medea suddenly remembered that Argus was on board. He was one of the Argonauts!

"The *Argo* was built long and narrow to ram enemy ships it might encounter, not to withstand storms. That's why we've stuck close to the shore of Turkey all this time instead of sailing directly across the middle of the sea!" Argus yelled back to Jason over the fierce sounds of the storm. "Our sail will be torn from its mast if this keeps up!"

"Furl the sail!" Jason commanded. Medea and Glauce watched as Zetes, Calais, and Heracles immediately leaped up from their benches to bind the huge, flapping sail to the tall pole that the two girls were gripping.

By now Medea's chiton was sopping wet, and the wind was whipping her hair around her like the snakes on Medusa's head! Pushing her hair out of her eyes, she glimpsed a startling sight beyond the three boys working at the sail. A small group of beautiful women were climbing up the anchor rope at the prow and practically slithering over the ship's railing! One of them reached into the ship, grabbed a square, flat object from under one of its benches, and then slipped back over the railing with her prize. With flips of their sparkly, scaly mermaidlike tails, the other women followed suit, diving into the sea and swimming away.

"Sea nymphs!" Medea yelled, pointing. "One

of them just stole something from under Heracles' bench!"

Heracles had been so busy furling the sail, and the other sailors so busy at their oars, that none had noticed the nymphs. Alerted now, some of the crew leaned over the railing, trying to track them and determine what they'd stolen.

"Oh no! Hylas is gone!" wailed Heracles. "Those nymphs took my shield!"

Tiphys was at the tiller trying to keep the ship on course, but he took in the situation in a quick glance. "Looks like they're heading for the mouth of a river at the city of Cius, Turkey!" he yelled over the storm.

"Hey, you shield-napping nymphs. Get back here!" Heracles bellowed. When the nymphs ignored him, he jumped into the heaving waves and swam after them.

"Bye!" he called back to the ship. "Sail on without me, Jason. I have to go find Hylas!"

"Those nymphs must be the troublemaking ones assigned to Eros!" Glauce yelled to Medea above the roar of the wind. "Do you think he made them crush on Heracles' shield too, so they'd steal it?"

"Maybe!" Medea yelled back, only then realizing Glauce was aware of Heracles' shield-crush. "Their job is to make trouble for the *Argo*. And luring Heracles away will mean he can't help Jason anymore!"

"We will miss your friendship and your strength in battle!" Jason called out to Heracles. He gave a formal farewell salute to the mega-strong mortal boy. "Good luck. And safe travels!"

Once they were safely through the storm, the Argonauts seemed disheartened and maybe a bit bored when no new adventures cropped up right away. Their low moods affected Medea and Glauce, too. Besides that, both girls were all wet again, which was not fun! Feeling grumpy, Medea watched Jason running around checking on things as she wrung seawater out of her chiton's skirt.

"I don't get why he was chosen as the leader of this quest," she said to Glauce. "You'd expect a leader to have super-incredible qualities—like Heracles' strength and battle skills, or Atalanta's speed, for example. Jason doesn't seem to have any qualities that really make him stand out."

"So what? Jason's still amazing!" Glauce argued.

Overhearing them, Jason nodded thoughtfully. "Thanks for the vote of confidence, Glauce, but Medea's right. I only wish I had the strength of Heracles, the speed of Atalanta, or the musical talent of Orpheus. My crew is *truly* amazing." He propped one foot on his bench and gazed out to sea, looking a little sad about his lack of talent.

"Oh, I didn't mean it like . . . I mean, I'm sorry I said that," Medea backpedaled, wringing out her drippy hair. "I'm sure you're doing your best."

"That's true, but *doing* my best isn't the same as *being* the best at something," Jason said matter-of-factly. "In spite of my lack of real skills, though, I'm proud as can be whenever one of my crew succeeds in using his or her special talents to help us all."

His expression filled with respect and awe for his crew as he turned to Orpheus and gestured grandly with one arm. "More music, maestro! As we sail, let's celebrate the members of our crew!"

Rallying at his words, the crew began rowing faster. The sail was hoisted, and Medea and Glauce went to sit upon the only empty bench. The one Heracles had formerly occupied.

While the ship picked up speed, Jason said to the Argonauts, "Please, why don't each of you sing out your name along with a few words about your amazing skills! Orpheus will turn your words into song, and we'll hope Apollonius will later enshrine them in his musical. That way the world will forever remember you as the extraordinary heroes you all are."

"Cool! I'll start things off," said Orpheus. Strumming his lyre, he sang, "Orpheus! I sing—it's my thing!" Then he looked at Atalanta. "Your turn!"

"Atalanta! I'm fast—never last!" she sang, which made everyone laugh.

"Tiphys! Ships aren't lost or late when I navigate," the pilot sang out.

Medea's head turned this way and that, memorizing the names of all the crew as more and more of them offered up funny but sincere rhyming descriptions of their talents. Soon everyone was smiling and in high spirits again.

Finally it was the figurehead's turn to sing about her special talent. Instead she put the crew on alert, singing, "I spy a king, in that beach boxing ring! Dead ahead."

Just then Medea's stomach rumbled. It was way past lunchtime!

7

Hungry

ALL EYES TURNED TOWARD BITHYNIA, A REGION
along the coast of Turkey. The figurehead was right.
A man wearing a crown and boxing gloves was on
the shore, jumping around on the sandy beach inside
a roped-off area that looked like a boxing ring.
Though he was the only person inside the ring, he
was punching the air in front of himself as if combat-
ing some invisible fighter.

A crowd standing outside the ring clapped their hands or banged clubs together now and then to applaud his actions. Nearby there were long tables heaped with food and drink. Medea licked her lips, practically drooling. Would they share?

At a signal from Jason, the sailors dragged their oars to slow the *Argo*. "Excuse me, Your Royal Highness," he called out. "We are on a long voyage and about to cross the Black Sea to Colchis. Do you have food you could spare?"

Hearing this, the king stopped punching the air to stare at the ship. After reading the name painted on its side, he thrust his arms wide. "The *Argo*! I've heard about you guys. Pheme's been spreading the word all over Earth about your quest. I suppose you've come to invite me, King Amycus, and the Bebryces people I rule to be part of the musical

Apollonius is going to make about your exploits?"

"If you'll let us dine at your table, Orpheus will certainly mention you and your hospitality in one of his songs," offered Jason.

The king planted his boxing gloves on his hips, appearing annoyed. "*Mention* me? Bah! I want a starring role! But I suppose I must do something outrageous to get more than a mention, right?" He cocked his head, thinking.

"Well, I—" Jason started to say.

"Fine. Here's my idea," the king interrupted him. "I hereby challenge one of your crew to a boxing match!"

The Argonauts just stared at him like he was batty, and given his odd behavior, Medea figured there was a very good chance that he was.

"Come on. Send your best fighter in here. I can

beat any of you," the king boasted, hopping around the boxing ring like a cricket and punching at the air. "And if I win, I get to throw the loser off a cliff. Include that in your little musical, why don't you? *Ha-ha-ha!* How's that for outrageous!"

"What if we win?" Jason countered. "Then can we share your food?"

"Sorry! It's fake food, meant only to lure worthy opponents here to fight me. You can't actually eat it, but I can offer you something else in the unlikely event that the opponent you send is victorious." The king snapped his fingers. "Royal accountant!" he called out. "Get over here, pronto!" A short man with a large mustache ran out from the crowd. Bowing to the king, he handed Amycus a cloth bag as big as his head. Its contents clinked and clanked when the king held it up to show the Argonauts.

"If against all odds your fighter wins, I will give you this bag of coins." The king then tossed the bag into a corner of the ring and started jumping around and punching Mr. Nobody again.

Murmurs flew among the Argonauts. "With all that cash we could buy food somewhere," said Tiphys. "That guy is too nutty to be trusted," warned Atalanta. "Mmm, nuts. I'm starving," groaned Orpheus.

"Any volunteers?" asked Jason, glancing around at his crew.

"Wasn't one of Ares' hero statues a fighter? The sailor Polydeuces?" Medea asked Glauce. Glauce's eyes lit up and she nodded.

Medea looked over at Jason and opened her mouth to suggest the sailor's name. But before she could, Glauce butted in, calling out, "Polydeuces! How about him?"

Grr. As usual, Glauce just *had* to beat her to the punch and take credit for her idea, thought Medea. She wished she'd been quicker to speak up!

"Well, I do have some experience," Polydeuces told Jason, bowing his head modestly.

Could this shy guy beat the king? He didn't have big muscles like Heracles, so Medea wasn't sure he was the best choice. However, Heracles was gone now, off in pursuit of his beloved shield, Hylas. So, cheered on by the crew, Polydeuces bravely left the ship and joined the king in the ring.

"Ha! All I'll have to do is sit on you to win this fight," the king joked upon seeing him. He looked large and menacing next to Polydeuces, who was but a boy, after all.

King Amycus leaped closer and immediately

struck the first blow with his right fist. Polydeuces ducked. Another blow came. Polydeuces did a somersault and rolled to the far side of the ring to avoid it. The king kept on swinging, and kept on missing. Polydeuces' strategy seemed to be to dance around the ring and dodge all the king's jabs until he wore him out. This strategy was working—but it was also making the king mad!

"Get over here! This isn't *dodge* boxing, ya know!" Amycus yelled, huffing and puffing.

"Yeah! Scaredy-cat! Booooo!" the crowd on the beach bellowed at Polydeuces.

The Argonauts shouted encouragements to him, though, even as the frustrated king charged him like an angry bull. Again Polydeuces hopped aside, so the king's fist only grazed his arm. The dodge knocked the king off-balance, and Polydeuces saw his chance. He struck a blow—a right hook to the king's jaw! *Pow!*

The king's eyeballs rolled around in his head like marbles, then he spun around three times and fell to the sand flat on his back. *THONK!*

"Woo-hoo!" Polydeuces gleefully kicked up his heels. He grabbed the bag of money and ran for the ship. Unfortunately, the Bebrycians turned out to be sore losers. They waved their clubs and stormed after him.

"Hooray for Polydeuces!" cheered the Argonauts. As soon as he had leaped aboard the *Argo*, the crew shoved off, leaving the angry mob behind. *Phew!* Orpheus played a sprightly tune on his lyre, making up lyrics about the boxing match as he went along, while the sailors rowed as fast as they could.

Once they were safe in the harbor again, Orpheus played a slower tune. Sliding their oars into the waves, the sailors relaxed a little, rowing at a more comfortable and rhythmical pace to the beat of his song.

Medea recalled Medusa questioning how Orpheus would prove useful on the quest. By now his worth was obvious. For one thing, he was keeping track of their exploits for Apollonius. But besides that, the rhythm of his songs—sometimes fast, sometimes slow—was helping the oarsmen keep time.

After sailing for several more hours with no sign of food onshore, Medea was so hungry she could've eaten the fleece itself if they'd had it. And that thing would probably taste awful! The crew was hungry also, judging from their constant chatter about what they'd eat if they could have anything their stomachs desired. "Fig pudding . . . olives and hummus . . . honey and bread."

In the late afternoon, as they entered the strait of Bosporus, the sailor in the crow's nest began pointing and shouting. "Café alert! *Fooood!*" At this, cheers went up from the ship.

A building came into view with a sign above its door that read GRAND OPENING! HUNGRY, HUNGRY HARPY CAFÉ #2. After dropping anchor, everyone except a few lookouts scrambled out of the ship onto shore. When they entered the café, three birdlike winged women with feathers and claws flapped over and introduced themselves.

"Welcome!" cawed one. "We're the Harpy triplets, best cooks from the Mediterranean to the Black Sea. I'm Aello, and that's Celaeno and Ocypete."

Jason cocked his head. "I think I've heard of you."

Aello nodded. "Our original location—now called Hungry, Hungry Harpy Café #1—is in the Immortal Marketplace, halfway between Earth and Mount Olympus. It's doing so well that we've just opened this second location."

"Congratulations!" Jason told her. "So, can you seat fifty-one of us for lunch?"

All three Harpies gasped.

"No?" said Jason, noting their dismay. "That's okay, we'll take our food to go, then."

"Collect orders from your crew and give them to us," commanded Celaeno.

"Yeah. And while you're at it, choose some of your crew to help us with the slicing, dicing, and peeling," added Ocypete.

While half-listening to this conversation, Medea and most of the Argonauts began to gaze around the café with a kind of horrified amazement. Its walls, and even its ceiling, were covered with unusual objects that, according to the small signs hanging next to them, had supposedly once been owned by immortals.

"Look at this dented can," Glauce whispered to Medea. "It says 'Zeus Juice' on it, but you can tell someone just hand-painted the word 'Zeus' onto a plain ol' juice can."

Medea gestured to the sign under a cute, sparkly pink spear. It read PROPERTY OF ARES. She lifted an eyebrow. "Pink? *Ares?* I don't *think* so!"

Glauce grinned. "Yeah, maybe Aphrodite would like that spear, but it is so *not* Ares." They giggled together, and it felt to Medea like they were more friends than enemies in that moment. If only it could always be that way.

"Psst!" When a thin man with gray hair hissed at

the crew, Jason, Medea, Glauce, Zetes, and Calais turned to look at him. "Run! Before you're robbed!" the man told them in a loud whisper. "This café is a terrible place to eat—not because of the food. Because of its thieving owners!" After taking a bite of his Greek pizza and a scoop of hummus, he poked his fork toward the Harpies. "Turn your back for two seconds and they'll steal the food you ordered right from under your nose!"

"That's not true, Phineas," tsked Celaeno, who had flown over to stand behind him. While his attention was on her, her sister Ocypete sneaked a clawed hand under his arm and snatched half of his pizza away! By the time he looked down and saw that slices were missing, both Harpies had disappeared into the kitchen, cackling with glee as they ate the purloined pizza themselves.

"See what I mean?" Phineas wailed to the Argonauts. "That's why I'm so skinny."

"We'll help you," Jason told him. "Zetes? Calais? Use those wings of yours to collect everyone's orders pronto, and round up some crew members willing to slice and dice. Cooking fifty-one meals ought to keep those thieving triplets occupied for a while."

"Got it," said Zetes. Then he nodded to Calais. "C'mon, bro, let's go."

Medea marveled at how gracefully and easily the two boys spread their wings and flitted around the café, quickly gathering lunch orders and delivering them to the Harpies. Must be nice to be able to fly! Soon those three bird ladies were so busy preparing the *Argo*'s big take-out order that Phineas was able to gobble down the last of his pizza in peace.

"Wow, thanks!" the skinny man told Jason as he finished all but the hummus. "In return for your help, let me warn you about a situation you're going to face on your voyage ahead. You'll need to watch out for an impossible passage."

"Im*pass*able passage?" echoed Medea, misunderstanding.

"Impossible, impassible, same difference," Phineas replied. "Look, I'll show you." Quickly he used his knife to form two tall piles of hummus on his plate, with an empty channel space between them. Gesturing to the piles, he said, "Pretend these are the two humongous rocks you'll find lurking on either side of this narrow passage in the Bosporus strait on your way to the Black Sea. They're dastardly blue rocks, each as big as three ships stacked one atop the other. Officially, they're named the Symplegades. But sailors call them other nicknames. Like Clashers, Smashers, Destroyers . . ."

Glauce's and Medea's eyes rounded. "That doesn't sound good," Glauce whispered.

"The thing about the Symplegades is that they can actually think, and they have a cruel sense of humor," Phineas went on. "If your ship tries to pass between them . . ." Using his fingertip, he pushed an olive representing the *Argo* into the empty channel separating his twin hummus mountains. *Whap!* With a mighty clap he smashed both mountains between his palms, turning them into a gooey sandwich with the flattened olive somewhere in the middle. "Then you, my friends, are history!"

Gasps went up from Medea and the others as they gazed upon the mess he'd made to indicate what would befall them and the *Argo*. "Is there another way through that channel?" Jason wanted to know.

"Nope. But I've got an idea how to trick those rocks," said Phineas, wiping the hummus and squished olive from his hands with a napkin. "So listen up."

8

Clasher Crushers

"HERE'S WHAT YOU DO," BEGAN PHINEAS. JASON and his shipmates leaned in, eager to hear how they might get through the Symplegades without ending up like the flattened olive. "Once you're close enough, send a dove flying between those two rocks," the skinny Phineas continued. "Count the seconds to see how fast they slam together trying to flatten it, and how long it takes them to move apart again afterward. Once you've calculated that, you'll know the exact right moment to sail between them!"

"Lunch is served!" the Harpies called to the crew just then. Fifty-one identical papyrus bags, each with the name of a crew member (plus Medea and Glauce) scribbled on its outside, were lined up on the food counter, ready to go.

Thanking Phineas and giving the Harpies the money Polydeuces had won from the boxing match, the Argonauts then left the café. After eating their fill back on the *Argo*, they sailed for the Symplegades with high spirits and full bellies.

Even when they spotted the two huge blue rocks in the sea ahead, they remained jolly, making jokes to keep themselves amused. "The color of those rocks really *clashes* with our armor," said Zetes.

Grinning, Atalanta added, "Yeah, and going

between them *strikes* me as a bad idea."

"I think this adventure calls for a *rock* 'n' roll song!" said Orpheus, making everyone laugh.

Their good mood changed to alarm, however, as they drew closer to the Symplegades. Abruptly the crew dragged their oars, causing Medea to grab the railing to keep from tumbling as the ship lurched. Looking to see why they were slowing, she saw that all around them broken wood timbers floated in the sea.

"Do you think those boards came from other ships destroyed by the Symplegades?" Calais ventured, bending over the railing to look. No one replied, but there was no need. The answer was obvious: *Yes!*

"Those two rocks are way bigger than Phineas

made them out to be," exclaimed Jason. "This may turn out to be our greatest trial yet."

Leaning against the rail up near the figurehead, Medea and Glauce had a good view of the treacherous Clashers ahead of them. "If Jason thinks we can squeak through the narrow passage between those rocks, then he's an Argo*NUT*!" Medea worried aloud.

The figurehead overheard her and moaned. "And since I'm at the front of the ship, I'll be first through. Woe is me. I've got a feeling I'm going to wind up in splinters!"

"They're right. This is a bad idea," Tiphys cautioned Jason.

"Rather than risk getting squished, we could lift the ship out of the water and carry it overland through Turkey," suggested Argus. "Athena designed the *Argo* with a shallow hull to make that possible. It'll be slow and tiring work, but at least we'll live to tell the tale."

Slow? Medea liked the sound of that. With the added time, maybe she could finally put that arrow in her pocket to good use and hopefully end this quest once and for all. She'd opened her mouth to vote for the idea, when they heard a crash.

BAM! A short distance ahead of the ship, the two blue rocks body-slammed each other. Afterward the crew was startled to hear deep laughter.

Atalanta pulled her oar from the water and placed it across her lap. "Was that . . . those rocks? *Laughing?*"

Sure enough, the rocks had voices. And they were guffawing thunderously, gleeful at the Argonauts'

approach. "C'mon through, sailors! We won't slam you. Promise!" called the tricky Symplegades.

No one believed them, of course.

Standing up, Jason propped one sandaled foot on the nearest bench and then eyed each of his crew members in turn, as if appraising their abilities. His glance lingered on a crewman with shaggy hair and eyeglasses. "Euphemus, you're the keenest-eyed guy I know," he said at last. "Think your aim is good enough to throw something directly between those rocks?"

Euphemus, who Medea recalled had been Dionysus's hero figure back at MOA, leaped from his bench a dozen rows up from the tiller. "Sure. What do you want me to throw?" he asked, looking around for a suitable object.

"Phineas suggested a dove. . . ." At Jason's words,

the gaze of every Argonaut lifted to search the sky. However, it was empty of birds right now.

Good thing, thought Medea. Even if there had been birds, hurling a live dove at the rocks seemed pretty mean to her. But it gave her an idea. She gestured at the bird pillows lying on the benches. "You may not have a real bird, but you do have—"

"I know, Jason! Why don't you throw the dove pillow that Lemnos girl gave you?" Glauce said, talking over Medea. Once again Glauce seemed to have guessed what she had been about to say and then stolen her idea. And once again there was no way to prove this without sounding whiny. When, oh when, would Medea learn to speak her ideas louder and faster?

"Good plan!" Jason approved.

Eagerly Glauce dashed to Jason's bench at the very

back of the ship, snatched up the pillow Hypsipyle had made, and hurried back up the aisle. Too late! Euphemus had already picked up the bird-shaped pillow from his own bench and headed with it to the front of the ship before she could reach him.

"Rats," muttered Glauce, plopping down on Euphemus's empty bench to glare at Jason's pillow in her lap. It was an easy guess that she didn't like that particular one simply because it had been embroidered for her crush by the flirty Hypsipyle.

"What's taking you so long?" the Symplegades rumble-mumbled to the ship's crew. "C'mon, there's a really cool surprise waiting on the other side of us. Just for you!"

"What a couple of liars!" Medea said under her breath.

Holding on to the sail rigging to keep his

balance, Jason stood on the raised area of the stern, where he had a good view of the entire ship deck and the sea ahead. "At your stations, Argonauts! Be ready to row hard and fast when I say." He'd spoken his order quietly to the crew. Because if the rocks could speak, they could probably hear, too, Medea figured.

After reaching the prow, Euphemus stood on deck to study the clashing rocks, his pillow in hand. When he judged the time right, he started turning in circles like a discus thrower. Once he was almost even with the figurehead, he stopped whirling and pitched the pillow high out over the sea ahead.

Medea's heart sang when the dove pillow soared through the gap between those two rocks. *Wait!* She'd gotten so caught up in this adventure, she'd forgotten that she didn't want these Argonauts to succeed! However, neither did she want anyone on board to be pulverized, so it was best that this dove plan work.

BAM! The rocks slammed together . . . and clipped the very tail end of Euphemus's bird-shaped pillow! Everyone gasped as the pillow's fabric tore and its tail stuffing puffed out.

"Row!" Jason urged his crew at that exact moment. "Head for those Clashers while they're still close together. They'll want to smash us between them, so they'll have to move apart when they see us coming. That's the moment we speed through."

"I am so doomed!" the ship's figurehead wailed. She covered her eyes with both her wooden hands.

Luckily, the ship zipped ahead and eased smoothly through the gap between the rocks. "Made it!" the Argonauts cheered, and Orpheus crooned:

"It was a tight squeeze,

But we got through with ease."

Realizing she'd survived, the figurehead opened her eyes and twisted her head around to cheer with the crew. "Woo-hoo!" But then her expression turned curious and she craned her neck toward the back of the ship. "Where'd your bench go, Jason?"

Huh? Everyone followed her gaze to the place where Jason's bench usually sat a few feet behind the tiller. It was gone! Somehow one of the jagged rocks had managed to clip the stern and knock the bench into the sea! Those two blue rocks were acting tickled pink as they body-slammed each other, smashing the bench between them. "Score!" they shouted. Their version of a high five, perhaps?

"A small price to pay!" Jason exclaimed, punching

a fist in the air. "We're getting close to our goal, Argonauts! Onward across the Black Sea to the kingdom of Colchis!"

Oh no! Medea stood as if frozen halfway between the stern and the ship's mast. Her mind raced, searching for a last-ditch effort that would stop Jason from reaching her dad's kingdom. There was the arrow in her pocket, of course. But time was running out. And even if she were able to prick Jason with it so that he began crushing on Glauce, would that girl really be able to convince him to give up his quest when he was so close to finishing it? Doubtful, she thought. Her shoulders slumped.

Hey! Maybe when no one was watching she could sneakily swim to the Colchis shore once the ship was near enough. Then she could warn her dad of Jason's approach and intent! But it seemed unlikely no one would notice her absence with all the Argonauts keeping careful watch over the ship and everyone on it, day and night. If she didn't do something fast, though, her dad was going to lose his prized fleece and be dethroned. According to Circe's prophecy, anyway!

Medea's blue eyes burned with frustrated, angry tears. *Uh-oh.* If she wasn't careful, she'd fry a hole in the hull of the ship and sink it! Hmm. Now *there* was an idea! Sure, it was kind of drastic, but what other choice did she have? They were close to a string of islands now, so everyone could swim to one of them. The crew would be okay.

Still, if anyone discovered she'd purposely sunk the *Argo*, Orpheus would probably write a song about it. And when Apollonius made his musical, she'd be the villain!

Her dad's whole kingdom was at stake, though. So sinking the ship it had to be! Medea had never before tried to bring forth her terrible power on purpose. But now she tuned out everything around her and searched her brain for thoughts that would be guaranteed to make her truly angry or immensely frustrated. Like Jason overthrowing her dad as ruler of Colchis! And Glauce one-upping her all the time! Within minutes her eyes glowed with fire. Hooray! It was working! Having put herself in a totally bad mood, she hunched her shoulders and rammed her fists into her pockets.

"Ow!" she cried out. The fire left her eyes and she jerked her left hand out of her pocket. The tip of Eros's mini arrow was stuck in her palm! Overcome by her anger, she'd momentarily forgotten about that arrow. And she'd accidentally pricked herself with it!

Shaking her arm, Medea flung the arrow from her hand, high over the ship's rail, where it fell into the sea and was quickly swept away. She glanced down at her palm and saw that the arrow tip had left a small, pink, heart-shaped mark on it. Strangely dizzy now, she stumbled, tripped on the rope coil, and pitched forward. She was falling overboard!

A strong hand grabbed her and pulled her back from danger. "Hey, watch out. You almost went swimming with the sea monsters. You okay?"

Medea looked up at her rescuer. "Jason?" His wavy chestnut hair suddenly looked glossier than before, his brown eyes more sparkly, his muscles bigger. He even seemed smarter somehow.

A happy, fizzy feeling filled her. "Whoa, I never noticed how cute you are!" she told him.

Instantly his cheeks turned red and he took a step backward.

"Sorry!" She slapped her uninjured hand over her mouth, realizing she had embarrassed them both. What was wrong with her? It was Eros's fault. Him and his dumb crush-causing mini arrow! *Ye gods!* She was pretty sure she was now crushing for the very first time. On her dad's enemy—Jason!

Unable to stop herself, Medea slid onto an empty bench and patted the seat beside her. Batting her eyelashes at him like she'd seen Hypsipyle do, she said, "Hey, come sit by me. I've got some ideas on how you can get that fleece." *What am I doing?* some part of her demanded to know as soon as the words left her mouth. But it seemed she was as helplessly besotted with Jason now as Heracles had been with his shield. Even though she knew deep down that she didn't truly *like*-like Jason, she couldn't stop herself from acting all goo-goo and gaga over him.

"Really?" Looking intrigued, Jason dropped onto the bench. His smile made Medea's heart go *ka-thump*.

Speaking of thumps, Glauce, who'd heard what Medea had just said to Jason and had been staring daggers at her, now thumped herself down on the bench on Jason's other side. "No offense, Medea, but why should Jason trust you?" Having gotten Jason's attention, Glauce went on. "There's something you should know about Medea. . . ."

Guessing what the girl was about to say, Medea gave her an urgent, warning shake of her head. However, Glauce ignored it and confided to Jason,

"King Aeëtes is her dad. He rules Colchis and owns that fleece you want."

Gasps went up from the crew, and Medea felt everyone's suspicion fall on her, just like at the beginning of the trip.

"Which is why I'm the best one to supply inside info on how to get the fleece," Medea declared quickly. "For instance, Jason, did you know my dad visits that Golden Fleece once a day, always in the evening? So you'll want to avoid trying to steal it then. And also, did you know that the serpent-dragon guarding it never sleeps? I can give you all kinds of helpful tips like that to help you steal the fleece, or at least avoid becoming dragon dinner."

"Hmph! If Medea has to pick a side, she'll help her dad," Glauce insisted. "No offense, Medea, but Jason shouldn't trust you."

"Let's trade her for the fleece!" someone in the crew suggested. Others chimed in, some in agreement with that idea and some disagreeing.

"You could try," said Medea, "but I suspect my dad loves that fleece more than me, so trying to trade me for it might not gain you anything. And do you really want Apollonius's musical to portray you acting so dishonorably?"

Jason eyed Medea in the same appraising way he'd looked at each of his crew members before picking Euphemus to hurl the pillow at the Symplegades.

Medea sat up straight. Holding his gaze, she said, "If you give me the chance, I pledge on the honor of my wand that I will help you get the fleece."

Glauce gasped, then grudgingly admitted to Jason and the others who were listening, "A pledge on your

174

wand is sacred to anyone who goes to Enchantment Academy. So I guess she really is telling the truth about helping with the quest."

Medea smiled, knowing she'd convinced her new crush and won this round with her frenemy. "So, Jason, here's the thing. My dad is super bossy. If he sees me tomorrow, he'll probably send me to my room to protect me from, uh, danger."

The real reason was that her dad would want to protect her from a fleece thief who had been prophesied to steal her heart. *Too late, Dad, Jason has already stolen it!*

"So anyway, I wouldn't be able to help you anymore if that happened. I'd better hide here on the *Argo* with the crew." Just after Medea said this, a vague memory of a previous plan to swim to shore and warn her dad about something flitted through her mind but then was gone. She smiled at Jason and went on talking, helping him plot her dad's defeat.

Around sunset the *Argo* dropped anchor near Colchis and Jason left the ship with Orpheus, Zetes, and Calais. As they went ashore, Medea and the others watched and listened from on board as Orpheus sang ditties to document their purpose.

> *"Jason is meeting Aeëtes the king.*
> *Here's hoping this visit will solve everything."*

"Not likely," said Glauce, eyeing Medea. "There are some things it won't solve, anyway. Like you crushing on my crush!"

"I can't help it. I got pricked with one of Eros's arrows," Medea protested. "So you'll just have to put up with me crushing on Jason till the arrow's magic wears off."

"What? Well, when's that going to be?"

Under the spell of the crush, Medea raised and lowered her shoulders. "Never, I hope!"

9
Three Tasks

MEDEA'S DAD MUST'VE HEARD THAT A SHIP had arrived, because he was waiting onshore with a group of guards and servants to meet Jason and the trio of crew members with him. Glauce and Medea watched from behind the ship's railing, hidden from King Aeëtes' view.

"Who are you? What's your business here?" the

king shouted out as Jason, Orpheus, Zetes, and Calais approached.

"I am Jason. Sent by King Pelias to get your fleece," Jason told him at once.

Medea gasped. She couldn't believe he'd come right out and admitted he was here to steal! She'd thought he would try to trick her dad or something.

"You're here to try to dethrone me, aren't you?" roared King Aeëtes as the boys came up to him.

Jason's eyes widened. "I have no plans to dethrone you. I only came for the fleece."

Her dad stroked his beard, then said, "My fleece? Sure, I'll give it to you."

"Huh?" Medea said, even more startled. She squinted, wishing she could make out her dad's expression. It might help her to figure out what he was thinking. He loved that fleece . . . right? He wouldn't just give it away to a stranger. And why was he acting so surprised about what Jason wanted? After all, Circe had *told* him a thief would come for the fleece. *Hmm.* What was he up to?

When her dad spoke to Jason again, it was in a jolly tone that worried Medea even more. "The fleece is yours!" said the king. "But only if you return tomorrow and complete three tasks I assign you before sundown." Orpheus sang from beside Jason.

> *"King Aeëtes of Colchis now boldly asks*
> *That our hero Jason tackle three tasks!"*

The king eyed the musician for a moment, then turned back to Jason. "By the way, you're not allowed to bring him or any of the guys from your crew to help you tomorrow."

"I bet Dad suspects that without the talents of his crew, Jason will have way less chance at succeeding at whatever tasks he's given," mused Medea.

"Stop saying that! Jason can too do stuff!" insisted Glauce.

Hmph! Her frenemy was so in like with Jason that she couldn't see past her own nose. Medea saw Jason as he truly was, however, despite her arrow-caused crush on him. She felt a spurt of anger at her dad. Why did he have to go and make Jason jump through so many hoops to get that fleece?

"But these tasks will probably be the most exciting part of our quest!" they heard Orpheus object to the king. "I need to be with Jason to compose songs about them, or Apollonius will be disappointed. He might even give up on the whole idea of a musical!"

King Aeëtes made a sour face, as if he'd been sucking on lemons. "Yes, I heard that that gossipy goddessgirl who writes for *Teen Scrollazine* has been spreading stories about some sort of musical. One that would celebrate your so-called quest to steal my property!"

Still safe behind the ship's rail, Medea whispered grumpily, "Her name's Pheme, Dad."

Her dad's head lifted and he glanced toward the ship. Worried for a second that he'd somehow over-heard her, Medea ducked and pulled Glauce down lower with her. After a few minutes they dared to peek over the rail again.

"All right, you can bring Orpheus, but he can't assist you," the king finally agreed. "So here's task number one, Jason. I've got a couple of bulls, and

I'd like you to get them to plow one of my fields in long, neat rows."

"Sure," Jason replied in a confident voice. "I'll get it done in a snap."

"Good," Glauce murmured to Medea. "Sounds like Jason has a plan."

"Maybe, but that task sounds too easy. There must be a catch," worried Medea.

"After you plow my field, I want you to plant some seeds in it for me," the king went on. For some reason he snickered as he handed Jason a small seed pouch.

"No problem," Jason replied easily.

"And then, if you survive, uh, I mean, if you manage to complete those first two tasks, your third and last one will be to fetch the Golden Fleece hanging in the grove beyond the field. If you can."

Now all the king's guards and servants were snickering too. Because everyone knew what guarded that fleece. A fierce serpentine dragon!

"Deal," said Jason, shaking the king's hand. Medea wondered if his quick agreement to the deal meant he had confidence in her ability to help him. At least where the dragon was concerned. By the time he returned to the ship, however, his confidence had vanished. He was more down in the dumps than the crew had ever seen him. "I have no clue how I'll get those tasks done in one day," he groaned.

"You don't have a plan, then?" Tiphys asked him.

"Not really. But I didn't want the king to know that." Jason sighed. "Without any crew to help, I guess I'll just have to wing it."

Before she had been pricked by Eros's arrow, Medea would have been delighted by his uncertainty.

Especially since it might've made him decide to give up his quest. But now she was only concerned for *him*. Somehow she had to help her crush succeed!

That night, unable to sleep, she paced up and down the *Argo*'s deck. Stopping near the figurehead, who was sleeping on guard duty, she happened to glance out across the sea and notice a stick lying on the beach. It was long and thin like a straw. *Hey! Did that stick just move?* As she watched, it gave a little twitch, then a jump, its tip sparkling with gold in the moonlight. Quickly it wrote something in the sand:

I AM YOUR WAND. COME GET ME!

"My magic wand!" Medea murmured excitedly. Currents in the sea must have helped it make its way here to Colchis, where it knew it would eventually find her. On silent feet she raced down the gangplank and picked it up. "What a faithful and wonderful wand you are," she told it. Back on the *Argo*, cradling her precious wand, she snuggled up on her coil of rope and fell fast asleep.

The next morning when she showed her wand to Glauce, the girl's only reply was, "What about mine? Did you look for it, too?"

Medea shook her head. "No, but I think mine came here because this is where I live. So maybe yours is looking for you back at Enchantment Academy."

"I hope so. Fat lot of good that does me right now, though," said Glauce. "Too bad wands only work for one person. Otherwise we could share yours."

"True." Relief filled Medea that Glauce wasn't going to be able to take over her wand like she did everything else!

Medea hurried to Jason at the stern of the ship. "My wand found me again," she said, waving it in

186

front of his face. "And even though my dad said none of the guys on your crew could help you do those tasks today, I can. Because I'm not officially on your crew and I'm not a guy, either."

"I could help too," said Glauce, who'd followed her. "For the same reasons."

"Me too," Atalanta chimed in from where she sat on her bench. "I mean, I *am* a crew member, but I'm obviously not a guy. All three of us could help and it wouldn't be breaking the rules."

Jason looked thoughtful. "The king would probably say I cheated if *anyone* gave me hands-on help. Technically speaking, he didn't say no *girls* could come, though. And your advice would be welcome." He looked at Medea. "But didn't you say he'd send you to your room if he knew you were here?"

"Well, my dad won't know any of us are with

you tomorrow if he can't *see* us!" So saying, Medea quickly waved her wand to do a cloaking spell that would render Glauce, Atalanta, and herself invisible.

"From all but Argonauts hide us three:
Glauce, Atalanta, and also me.
And let no one in Colchis hear us speak
While the Golden Fleece we seek."

"Okay, let's go," said Jason. "My first task is to plow up a field."

Medea nodded, aware that he and the others could still see her. "I know which one my dad meant. It's a couple of acres that have never been plowed before. I'm guessing it'll take all morning, but with two strong bulls it should be doable. We can worry about the other two tasks later."

When they arrived at the field, Orpheus sang,

"In the king's field are two bulls snorting fire.

Taming them to start plowing is Jason's desire."

His description of the bulls was totally accurate, but they did not look interested in being tamed. *Snort! Snort!* Fire was blasting out of their nostrils! After pawing the ground, they suddenly charged. Jason, Medea, Glauce, Atalanta, and Orpheus jumped out of the way just in time to avoid getting trampled.

"Your dad is so mean!" Glauce said to Medea.

"Never mind the bulls. I'll just pull the plow myself," Jason declared. But when he tried to lift the plow, he discovered it was much heavier than expected. "It's made of stone instead of wood! Those strong bulls could probably drag it, but I can't."

"If only there were some way to protect you from their fiery snorts so you could work with them," said Glauce.

Maybe there is, thought Medea. Looking around, she spied a clump of a yellow-flowering charmed herb that she'd remembered grew in patches in this field. After plucking a clump of it, she showed it to Jason and Orpheus. "My aunt Circe sometimes makes a cream for me from this herb," she told them. "I use it to protect other people from my, er . . . from getting sunburned."

Oops, she'd almost given herself away! She wasn't at all sure how Jason would feel about her if he knew how her eyes flashed and sometimes sunburned people or melted stuff when she got mad. She wanted her crush to *like* her, not fear her! Luckily,

Glauce and Atalanta had moved to the edge of the field and were discussing the bulls, so they hadn't overheard. Otherwise Glauce might've thought to reveal Medea's deep, dark secret.

Kneeling, Medea quickly ground the herb she had picked between two stones until it was a paste. "Here, Jason. Rub it on your skin, shield, and sword. It should protect you from the bulls' fire."

"Thanks," said Jason, taking the herb mixture and doing as she suggested.

"Anything for you," Medea assured him in a goo-goo, lovey-dovey voice that she hardly recognized as her own. When Orpheus looked at her curiously, she cringed. If he noticed she was crushing on Jason, would he write a song about it? How embarrassing would that be!

After Jason had rubbed the cream on himself and

his armor, he had no problem harnessing the bulls despite their fiery snorting. In no time at all they had helped him plow the entire two acres into long, neat rows ready for planting. And he didn't get a bit scorched!

Task completed, Jason unharnessed the two bulls and they wandered away from the newly-plowed field to graze in the distance. Medea smiled at Jason, saying, "Now for task number two."

Jason loosened the pouch of seeds he'd gotten from the king, which he'd tied to the waist of his armor. Looking rather pleased with himself for having managed task one, he casually tossed the pouch from one hand to the other.

A thrill zipped up Medea's spine when he glanced over at her and smiled. "All I have to do is plant these in the soil I plowed," he said. "Easy-peasy." Eagerly he took off running up and down the long rows the bulls had made, sprinkling the seeds. Within minutes he finished the task. As he ran triumphantly back across the field to Orpheus and the girls, he threw out his last few remaining seeds.

"Done!" he crowed happily.

Medea peered at the seeds he'd dropped a few yards behind him. "Ye gods! Those aren't seeds, they're—" Before she could say "dragons' teeth," Atalanta spoke up.

"Uh . . . Jason, you might want to turn around," she said.

When Jason did, he saw what the others had already seen. Hundreds of metal warriors were magically sprouting up in rows from the "seeds" he'd planted. *Clank! Clank!* They turned and eyed Jason, then grinned, showing jagged metal teeth.

"Crush! Kill! Destroy!" chanted the warriors. Like robots, they began marching single file toward Jason and the others up and down the long, straight rows. Only when they reached the end of one row would they turn up the next.

The tin men didn't seem to understand that they could've just stepped over the rows of dirt to reach Jason faster, Medea realized. So, however fierce and powerful they might be, maybe they weren't so bright.

"Those metal men are a little goofy in the roofy," observed Atalanta, echoing Medea's thoughts.

"Yeah, they must have rocks in their heads instead of brains," added Glauce.

That gave Medea another idea. She picked up a big rock and handed it to Jason. "Quick! Throw this at one of them."

"Won't that just make them mad?" he asked her.

Glauce looked at Medea worriedly. "Yeah, they might attack. Jason could get hurt!"

For once Jason actually seemed to notice Glauce. "Thanks for caring," he told her. And then he gave her a warm smile.

"You're welcome," she said shyly.

Jason gazed at her in confusion, as if trying to figure something out.

Atalanta rolled her eyes at him. "Seems like I'm the only girl on the *Argo* who *isn't* crushing on you. Now, get out there in that field and do some crushing yourself!"

At the mention of girls crushing on him, Jason actually blushed! But then he grinned at Glauce. She smiled back hopefully, wearing a sweet expression that Medea couldn't recall ever seeing on her face before.

Orpheus began murmuring yet another song under his breath. Could it be about Glauce crushing? Medea wondered. What was going on here? Was Jason falling in like with Glauce? Anger welled up in her. She wanted to stomp her feet and yell, *Pay attention to* me, *Jason! I'm the one helping you with your tasks!* Her eyes began to heat up. *Uh-oh!* She closed them tight and took several deep breaths to calm herself, so as not to give anyone here a sunburn. Or worse!

Regaining control of herself, she opened her eyes just in time to see Jason throw the rock she'd given him into the middle of the warriors. As she'd hoped, they clattered to a stop.

Eyeing one another accusingly, they began to argue. "Hey! Why did you throw that rock at me?" "What? I didn't do it!" "He did." "Liar! Liar! Tin pants on fire!" Soon they started throwing punches.

With each smack the bolts holding their parts together loosened. Eventually those bolts broke. And one by one the metal monsters began to fall apart. It wasn't long before they were reduced to a big pile of rubble!

Sounding joyful, Orpheus sang a loud victory song:

"Jason fought creatures who were silly dolts.
Now they're twisted metal and old broken bolts."

"Thanks, Medea! Two down. One task to go," said Jason.

His praise buoyed her, but Medea was still bothered by the way he and Glauce had gazed at each other. There was no time to dwell on that right now, though.

"You still have to defeat the serpent-dragon that guards the fleece," Atalanta noted.

Jason, Orpheus, and the three invisible girls

moved to the end of the field where a grove enclosed by a wrought-iron fence stood. A half dozen fountains with dancing waters surrounded the enormous oak that grew at the center of the grove. And from a branch of that oak hung the fleece, gleaming bright gold in the sunlight.

"Only Medea and I will go in," said Jason, taking charge. "The rest of you should stay back. No sense taking chances. That dragon looks like a killer. And anyway, you'll be able to see what's going on from behind the fence.

None of the others even tried to argue with him, not even Glauce since she feared creepy serpentine things. The dragon did look fearsome! It was turquoise and scaly, with a pointed fin rising from its forehead and bat wings at its shoulders. Its head rested high in one of the oak tree's leafy branches and its long, serpentine tail was wound around the tree's trunk. Medea was glad to go with Jason, though. Anything to help her crush!

Creak! The gate squeaked as she and Jason entered and tiptoed inside. The dragon shifted and snuffled but didn't look their way.

Jason and Medea crept toward it cautiously. Medea had never been this close to it before. Glancing away from the creature for just a moment, she spotted her dad's jewel-studded chair at the far side of the tree. She frowned at it, imagining him sitting there every evening to gaze adoringly at his fleece.

"Sleeping on the job. Hmph! What a lazy dragon," whispered Jason.

"Careful," Medea warned him. "It's likely to be a trick. Like I told you, that dragon *never* sleeps."

"But its eyes are closed. Maybe we can just grab the fleece and sneak away?" He took a step in the dragon's direction.

Medea was about to question the wisdom of that plan when she heard someone singing softly. Afraid for Jason, Orpheus had begun quietly crooning outside the gate, though not with his usual gusto:

> *This dragon looks fierce,*
> *Who knows what it'll do?*
> *Will Jason, our leader,*
> *Wind up barbecue?"*

She frowned back at Orpheus. "Shh!" she hissed. But it was too late. Having heard him, the dragon went on full alert. Roaring out a fiery blast, it swiftly uncurled from the tree trunk and lunged at Jason with its saw-blade teeth bared!

Medea gasped. Was her crush indeed about to be barbecued . . . and *eaten*? They both jumped back. Thinking fast, Medea ran to the walled edge of the closest fountain. There she grabbed a green flagon and used it to dip water from the fountain. Quickly she whipped out her gold-tipped laurel wand. A bluebird fluttered near and sat upon the dry end of her wand curiously, not realizing she was there. For a moment she'd forgotten she was invisible to all but her small group.

The bird flew off, startled when she tapped her wand against the outside of the flagon. She did so six times, once for each letter in the word "dragon," while murmuring a simple spell that would trans-form the water into a magic potion:

"Potion in this flagon

Bring sleep to that dragon!"

In the distance she heard Orpheus softly repeating her words to himself. Would her spell wind up in the musical? Who knew?

Medea rushed the potion over to the dragon. "No! Give it to me," Jason called out over the creature's roars. "I need to do each task myself."

"Oh, right!" Medea thrust the flagon into Jason's hand just as the dragon lunged. Angry green puffs exploded from its snout. Its forked red tongue flicked and its jaws opened wide. Somehow it seemed to sense she was there even though the bird had not. Would it swallow her and Jason both whole? She hugged herself tight, fearing the worst.

Splat! Jason splashed the sleeping potion in the dragon's face.

Instantly it jerked backward, its red eyeballs crossing and a goofy grin spreading across its turquoise, scaly face. The dragon swayed uncertainly, and then toppled to the ground. *BOOM!* With its head resting on a thick root, it curled its tail around the oak's trunk and started to snore. Once the dragon was no longer a threat, Orpheus, Atalanta, and Glauce opened the gate and ran into the grove.

Standing under the tree, Jason jumped, reaching for her dad's treasured cape. He missed. He jumped again. And missed again. Atalanta tried giving him a boost, but it was no use.

"It's too high!" Jason declared.

They all looked around the grove. At the exact same moment, Jason and Medea pointed to the king's jeweled chair. "We can use that!" they both exclaimed. Since it would've been breaking the king's rule for Orpheus to help, he could only watch as Jason and the three girls dragged the heavy chair over to the tree and positioned it below the branch with the fleece.

Jason grabbed a long stick from the ground, then climbed to stand on the chair's seat. *Whap!* He swung the stick at the fleece. Yet another miss. He was still too low. In a risky move, he climbed higher to stand with one foot on each of the chair's sturdy arms, while the girls helped him balance. *Whap!* In one try he finally knocked that Golden Fleece from the branch! When it dropped to drape neatly across the chair's high back, he clambered down. "Got it!" he shouted.

Just then, they heard a noise from the far end of

the grove and saw the flash of armor. "Someone's coming! My dad's guards," warned Medea.

"Let's go, just in case they try to back out of our deal," said Glauce.

Unfortunately, when Jason tried to grab the fleece, it wouldn't budge. "It's stuck, caught on the chair's jewels!" he informed them. Orpheus tried to help loosen it, but then said, "It'll rip if we pull harder."

As the sounds of clanking armor drew closer, the guards spotted them. "Look! Jason has a guy from his crew helping him. Tell the king that there's cheating afoot. Deal's off! Return the fleece!"

"Oh no!" said Medea. Had they been cheating? Depends on how you defined the exact time this third task ended. She had a feeling both sides would forever disagree about that, but her crush on Jason kept her firmly on his side in this matter.

"We'll just have to take the chair with us. C'mon!"
she hissed. So Jason, Orpheus, and the girls hefted
the chair with the fleece between them and ran
through the gate. Then all five made a break for
the *Argo*.

10

Escaping

W E DID IT! WE GOT THE FLEECE!" JASON proclaimed jubilantly once they were back on the ship and Medea had reversed her spell, making Atalanta, Glauce, and herself visible again. It took Jason about ten minutes to carefully loosen the precious fleece from the king's chair and store it in his leather sack for safekeeping. Then, as the ship shoved off, he marched to the stern with the chair and set it in the same spot his old bench had occupied before the Symplegades smashed it. Plopping himself down in the seat of the fancy chair, he smiled, looking very proud of himself.

"So now what?" Glauce asked him. "Are you going back to Iolcus to give the fleece to King Pelias? Think he'll really give you back your dad's kingdom if you do?" Her questions reminded Medea that even though the quest for the fleece was over, Jason still had other goals to accomplish.

"After all we've been through to get it, he'd better!" said Jason. "Listen, I'll drop you girls off at your school. It's not on our way, but it's the least we can do to repay you for your help."

Glauce pouted slightly, looking unhappy at the prospect of being parted from him. But Medea only nodded. Jason had won. Her dad had lost.

Though the effects of Eros's arrow made her happy for Jason, she felt heartsick that she'd betrayed her dad. Would he be dethroned now, as Circe had prophesied? She hoped not! It hardly seemed fair that by helping Jason's dad get *his* kingdom back, Medea might've caused her own dad to lose his kingdom!

The sun soon turned bright orange as it sank lower, sending strands of pink and purple along the horizon. Standing at the tiller, Tiphys gazed at the darkening sky, then bent to study a mysterious dotted scroll he held. When he noticed Medea staring at him curiously, he explained, "It's a star chart showing heavenly objects. By comparing the positions of stars and planets to the location of land formations we pass, I'm able to navigate the ship."

"Interesting!" Medea said in fascination. If she

were going to be on the ship longer, she would have liked to learn more.

"Danger!" the crewman in the crow's nest suddenly shouted. "King Aeëtes is in pursuit!"

"Now that's what I call a dramatic announcement! Good job!" the figurehead praised him.

All heads turned to look back across the water toward Colchis. *Yikes!* It was true! Medea's dad was indeed sailing behind them. Euphemus, Atalanta, and Calais sent warning arrows arcing across the sky toward the king's ship. But still it plowed straight ahead, gaining on them.

She should've known her dad would come after the *Argo*, thought Medea. After all, his guards would have informed him that Jason and Orpheus had cheated in getting the Golden Fleece, even though that wasn't strictly true in her opinion. Crouching low to make sure she couldn't be seen from the king's ship, Medea's eyes scoured the *Argo*, searching for anything that might help head off a battle. "I know! Can I have someone's bird pillow?"

Immediately Glauce grabbed Jason's pillow and handed it to her. "Are you going to throw it overboard?" she asked hopefully.

"Something like that. I . . . ," began Medea. Then her mouth snapped shut. For once, she wasn't going to hint at her idea so Glauce could take charge of it as her own. Instead, using her wand, Medea zapped the pillow into a likeness of the fleece.

Handing it to Jason, she said, "Tell my dad that this is his precious fleece. And then let him see you toss it overboard," she instructed. "Looking for it ought to slow him down."

"Good idea!" Jason jumped up to stand on the

seat of the jeweled chair. Holding the pillow-turned-fleece high in one fist, he shouted to the Colchis ship. "Here! You can have your fleece back!" Then he drew back his arm and sent the fake fleece soaring. It angled high before dropping into the sea about halfway between the two ships. *Splash!*

Behind them, King Aeëtes' ship raced up to the spot where the fake fleece had splashed down. But the waterlogged fleece had quickly sunk beneath the waves. As the king's ship came to a stop, the Argo sailed swiftly onward.

"They're fishing around for it with spears and nets," called the crow's-nest crewman moments later.

"The king and his men must think it's really the fleece!" the figurehead rejoiced.

Jason nodded happily. "By the time they rescue it and figure out it's a fake, we'll be long gone."

As the Argonauts made their getaway, Medea sat on Heracles' former bench and watched the distance between the *Argo* and her dad's ship widen until the king's ship was only a tiny point on the distant horizon. She was filled with heartache. Number one: She had betrayed her dad. And number two: Her crush was obviously in like with Glauce, not *her*. Even now Jason was gazing fondly at Glauce as the two of them happily chatted together.

Turning away from them, Medea stared unhappily out to sea. A minute or two later she was startled to look up and see Jason standing beside her. "I just wanted to say thanks, Medea. I couldn't have gotten the fleece without you. I know that."

She smoothed her hair and jumped up. "Glad to help," she said brightly.

"You really saved my bacon back there in Colchis,

and then again when your dad came after us on his ship," Jason went on. "We couldn't have succeeded without your fast thinking. The whole ship is grateful to you."

Medea beamed at him. It felt good to receive credit and praise for her ideas. Especially since, through a large part of their journey, Glauce had either put her ideas down or claimed them as her own. Thinking on this, she suddenly knew she'd been mistaken about Jason's lack of skill.

"You know, what I said about you before was wrong. You're actually a really good leader," she told him earnestly. "And leading others well takes skill."

He cocked his head at her. "Oh?"

"Yeah, I can see now that it took smarts to choose just the right crew and to figure out everyone's capabilities," Medea explained. "And I truly admire how you've encouraged and brought out the best in all of us throughout the voyage."

Hearing her, the other crew members nodded in agreement. "She's right." "It's true." "You let all of us shine as bright as the fleece, Jason!" various members exclaimed. The figurehead joined in. "Hooray for Jason!" it called out.

"Hip, hip, hooray!" everyone shouted. This time Jason was the one beaming. And Medea was happy for him. But her happiness soured when Glauce came over and slipped her hand into his.

Hmph. Just when Medea had decided Jason was a good judge of character, he showed bad judgment in liking Glauce! Why couldn't he see her flaws like Medea had come to see them? She remembered the saying "love is blind." So maybe crushing made you blind to the flaws of the one you were crushing on.

Whatever. Medea was seriously starting to wish her own crush feelings would go away!

The wind picked up a few minutes later, turning the waves choppy. Another of Poseidon's storms blew in, and it kept the whole crew busy for the rest of the evening. That godboy must be showing his displeasure over the outcome of the quest, thought Medea. Well, despite Jason's praise, she wasn't totally satisfied either. She was really worried about what might be going on back home in Colchis. Had her dad already lost his kingdom—the only home she'd ever known?

After the storm stirred up the sea, it was easy to catch fish. Medea set aside her worries as all on board celebrated their bounty with a seafood feast. Spirits were high among the crew as they went to sleep that night.

Three days later on Saturday, the morning dawned bright and sunny. When Medea woke, the *Argo* was heading straight for Aeaea. She could already see the red and black flags of Enchantment Academy whipping in the breeze at the top of the hill!

Upon reaching the school, the *Argo* paused just long enough to drop off Glauce and her. Jason had gone out of his way to take them home, and so was understandably eager to rush onward and deliver the fleece to King Pelias at Iolcus, back where this whole quest had started. Waving farewell to the Argonauts, the two girls watched them sail away.

"Medea! Glauce! Are you okay?" Circe was back from MOA and came running down to the shore to greet them, having seen the ship. With evident relief she hugged them both while frowning after Jason and his crew as if suspecting they'd been responsible for the girls' disappearance. "I only returned to EA minutes ago myself," she told them. "That's when I found out you hadn't been here all week as I'd believed. But I'm sure I wanded you here from the Hero-ology classroom last Monday. So what happened? How did you wind up aboard the *Argo*?"

As the three of them took the stone steps up the embankment to the school, Medea and Glauce explained. Once they'd made it clear that Jason hadn't kidnapped them, Circe calmed down. "You girls must be hungry. Come, most of the students are still at breakfast. I'll get you something to eat."

The minute they entered the cafeteria, a girl from school ran up to Glauce, holding out a wand. It leaped from the girl's hands to Glauce, who caught it gratefully. "You found me!" she said, hugging her wand like a long-lost friend.

Circe brought them breakfast, listening in as Glauce eagerly told everyone her version of the quest. Medea grew more and more anxious when every sentence her frenemy spoke began with "I." She didn't even mention Medea at all unless it was a thinly veiled put-down.

Still under the effects of Eros's crushing spell, Medea picked at her food as Glauce gleefully revealed that she and Jason were crushing. Medea couldn't help feeling sad and jealous of their happiness.

But when Glauce spoke about stealing the fleece, Circe's eyes narrowed. "Medea, come with me, please," she instructed sternly. Once they were standing together at the side of the cafeteria, Circe folded her arms. "Okay, what's going on with you?" she asked. "I know there must be some reason you helped those Argonauts get the fleece. Or is Glauce fibbing about that?"

Medea sighed, and a tear leaked from the corner of one eye. "I'm sorry, Aunt Circe. I've made a big fat mess of things. Not on purpose, though." She held out her palm to display the tiny heart-shaped spot still visible there. "See, I pricked my hand on one of Eros's crush-causing arrows. It made me start liking Jason—a *lot*. That's why I helped the Argonauts get Dad's fleece. Because I was crushing on Jason. I still am, even though I don't want to be. Liking somebody can be really miserable, you know?"

"And Glauce?"

"She's crushing on him too, only I think her crush is for real," said Medea.

Circe patted her shoulder, saying mysteriously, "Don't worry. Go back to your breakfast. I'll fix this."

While Medea returned to her table, Circe ducked into the cafeteria kitchen. A few moments later she was back with two tall glasses of lemonade. She held them out to Medea and Glauce. "You must be thirsty," she told them. "Drink up!"

Having been at sea for so long, the two girls really were thirsty. They quickly drained their glasses. Afterward Medea sat up straighter, frowning. She felt different somehow.

"And so then Jason smiled at me . . . ," Glauce was saying.

Hey! Hearing Glauce speak of her crush didn't hurt now! And when Medea thought of Jason, her heart didn't go *ka-thump* anymore. Sure, she still admired him as a great leader and a good guy. However, the intensity of her feelings had altered. She wasn't crushing on him!

Why the change? Medea glanced at her aunt, who smiled a secret smile and eyed the now-empty glass by Medea's plate. Of course! That lemonade! Circe must have put some kind of anti-crush potion in it. Maybe the lemon-flavored potion had somehow soured her crush on Jason. Hooray! At last the *crush*ing unhappiness of liking a boy who didn't like her back had been lifted. She felt pounds lighter!

"Oh, I wish you guys could meet Jason. He is *sooo* adorbs!" she heard Glauce say. Ha! Obviously *her* crush hadn't soured one bit! Circe's potion must only work on the kind of crush that was magically caused, like Medea's had been.

Once breakfast ended, Medea and Glauce went to shower and change. After they'd gotten fresh uniforms from the supply room and put them on, they headed for Circe's office.

Along the way Medea noticed a poster in the hall announcing that the Magicasters Club tryouts would be held in the open-air auditorium after school on Monday. Up to three new members would be invited to join those already in the club. Other posters like this one had been hanging all over EA for the past few weeks. Before either girl could remark on the notice, Circe appeared. "Time for me to magic you home," she said to Medea.

"Please," Medea said to her aunt, "I know I have to go home and face the music. But first can you prophesy my future? Will Dad forgive me when he finds out what I did?"

"I'll try," Circe agreed. Her eyes took on that familiar faraway look, and when her vision came, she told Medea, "You will soon meet someone wise beyond her years. She will suggest something you should *undo* and something you should *do*." With that confusing (and unhelpful!) prophecy, Circe waved her wand and sent Medea traveling back to Colchis.

But not before Glauce got in a few last words of criticism. "No offense, Medea, but you're holding your wand the wrong way again!"

Medea barely had time to roll her eyes, and then she was back at her dad's palace. Finding him seated on his grand throne, she nervously wished Circe's prophecy had been more helpful (and hopeful!) about her future. Still, she was so happy to see her dad that she ran over to him at once. "Dad!"

"Medea! You're safe!" he boomed, jumping up to hug her tight. "I was so worried about you when Circe sent word that you'd been missing all week and had only just returned to the Academy this morning."

When he let her go again, she said, "I'm sorry! There was an accident at Mount Olympus Academy and I got magically sent to . . . to the *Argo*." She took a deep breath. Then, before she could lose her courage, she confessed all. "And I helped the Argonauts steal the fleece! I tried to stop them at first, but then I fell under a boy-liking spell caused by one of Eros's arrows, and helped Jason and his crew instead," she said in a rush.

Her dad stared at her in surprise and practically fell back onto his throne. By the time she'd filled in the details of all that had happened since she'd accidentally found herself caught up in the quest, the king's expression had turned thoughtful. "No mortal can fight the power of an arrow from the immortal Eros. I'm just glad you're home safe."

"Really? But what about your fleece! And your fancy jeweled chair! And your guards said our side cheated."

"Bah! Cheat schmeat. A cape and a seat. I admit I was more attached to them than I should have been. But they are only things, and I can get new ones. Daughters, on the other hand?" His eyes glistened with tears. "You're my one and only. And you've made me proud. Not only did you come up with some clever ideas to help Jason on that quest, you also showed true courage both in helping him and in admitting to me just now what happened. You've taken care of yourself and others, too. Seems you're capable of much more than I've given you credit for."

Medea smiled, practically glowing with happiness. Then, remembering her earlier worry, she said, "But I thought that if you lost the fleece, you'd be dethroned. Meaning you'd lose your kingdom." She looked around. "Only that hasn't happened," she added, seeing that things seemed pretty much the same as always.

Her dad smiled at her fondly. "Circe and I *believed* the prophecy meant I'd lose my kingdom. After hearing your tale, I realize that it only said I would lose my *throne* to Jason, which indeed I did. You and he took the small throne I left in the grove!"

"Oh!" They shared a laugh at this.

Medea smiled even more broadly, feeling happier than she had in some time. But her joy dimmed when she remembered that on Monday she'd have to go back to school, and everything would be just the same as before her big adventure this week, with her living here and having to be whisked back and forth each day. Unless . . .

She gave her dad a sidelong glance. He was in a good mood right now. Should she find out if he'd at least consider letting her board at school like the other EA students? After all, she had proved she could take care of herself on a dangerous quest. She took a deep, fortifying breath, then opened her mouth to ask. But before she could utter a word, a royal servant burst into the room and called him away to tend to some problem at the far end of the realm. After giving her another quick hug, her dad was off, not to return until late Sunday night. Medea sighed, watching him scurry away with his attendant.

She went over to the window seat where she'd

eavesdropped on Circe and her dad a week ago and sat on it, feeling droopy. "Well, you missed your chance," she muttered to herself. "Looks like nothing's going to change around here."

But what could she do about that?

11
Magicasters

WHEN MEDEA RETURNED TO ENCHANTMENT Academy on Monday morning, the quest of the *Argo* was the talk of the whole school. And Glauce was making sure she and Jason were the stars of the tale.

"So when we were on the quest, I came up with the idea to throw the dove-shaped pillow through those terrifying Clasher rocks!" Glauce said to students gathered around them in the hall as they went to first-period classes.

Medea ground her teeth. *Grr.* As usual, Glauce had left her out of the story. Over the course of the morning, if Glauce ever bothered to include her in any descriptions of the quest, she made Medea's actions seem silly or misguided.

And, as usual, Medea let her. Because if she butted in to tell the true story, she knew she'd come off sounding boastful and nitpicky. *Hey, cutting me down doesn't build you up, you know*, Medea wanted to tell her frenemy. But Glauce would only pretend to be wounded by her accusation. Or to not understand what she meant.

Many students seemed especially fascinated with Glauce's famous new crush, Jason. Even though

Medea was no longer crushing on him herself, it still hurt that Glauce took every opportunity to rub it in that Jason liked her and not Medea.

"I'm pretty sure Orpheus even wrote a song about Medea crushing on Jason. So embarrassing for her!" Glauce said when they were all in the cafeteria lunch line.

Finally Medea couldn't take any more. "Anybody would start crushing if one of Eros's arrows struck them," she protested in her defense.

"Yeah, that's true. It wasn't Medea's fault," put in a girl standing in line with them. Her name was Arete, and she was in the Magicasters Club. Medea knew her, but not all that well. Still, she smiled Arete's way, grateful that the girl had stood up for her.

Glauce shrugged. "Well, regardless, Apollonius is

bound to put Medea's hopeless crush in his musical." She smiled as if she found this amusing.

Medea noticed that others were now giving Glauce looks, too. *Disapproving* looks. Like maybe they felt that she wasn't being fair to Medea.

"Anyway," Glauce went on. "From the letter Jason sent me last night by messenger pigeon, I can tell you that the *Argo*'s adventures continue. On their way to Iolcus, the crew barely avoided the lure of Sirens perched on some jagged rocks along the shore." Having successfully captured her listeners' attention again, she smiled. "Good thing, too, because those Sirens' idea of fun is to sing so beautifully that passing ships will sail closer and wreck on those jagged rocks!"

Gasps sounded. The students in line hung on Glauce's every word as they filled their trays and then went to sit in the cafeteria. By the time Medea followed others to the long table they ate at, she could only find a seat at the far end. Glauce was at the other end—the *head* of the table—like a queen holding court.

"And that's not all," Glauce told her spellbound listeners. "The Argonauts encountered this enormous mechanical giant named Talos on the island of Crete. It blocked their way home, threatening to hurl great boulders down on them. But guess how they foiled him?"

"How?" asked several students.

"By pulling a nail from his ankle. That caused the oil inside Talos—which was what kept the machinery parts inside him running—to drain out. And then he fell into the sea!" crowed Glauce.

"Hi, okay if I sit here?" someone asked. Medea looked over to see that Arete was standing next to her with her lunch tray by the single empty seat at the long lunch table.

"Sure," Medea said in surprise.

Once Arete was seated, she glanced toward Glauce at the other end of the table, then looked at Medea. "Did she really do what she claims she did on the *Argo*?" she asked quietly. "Just asking, since you were there and all."

For once someone was asking for *her* side of the story. Remembering how Glauce had taken credit for things she shouldn't have, Medea wanted to blurt out the total, brutal truth. Still, she didn't want Arete to think that she was spiteful or that she was trying to take all the credit herself!

"Some of it," Medea said tactfully.

"Hmph. That's what I figured," said Arete, seeming to take Medea's meaning, even though she hadn't exactly spelled it out.

"Thanks for sticking up for me in the lunch line," Medea added.

Arete shrugged and cocked her head toward Glauce. "I don't like how she always teases people and puts them down. But in a weirdly nice way so that most of the time it almost seems like she's helping them. Some people really know how to one-up you, you know?"

"Yes, I do know," Medea replied in surprise. She'd been so focused on her own feelings that it hadn't occurred to her that others might actually see Glauce the same way she did.

"I used to hang out with her some," Arete admitted

as she ate. "But she was never very nice to me. And after she was mean to me for, like, the millionth time, I decided I didn't have to put up with it. So I decided to *undo* my friendship with her. And to *do* stuff I wanted to do that she said I couldn't."

Huh? Medea's mouth dropped open. *Undo? Do?* Those were the very words Circe had prophesied that someone wise beyond her years would speak to her! Well, if Arete was in Magicasters, she must be smart, which was kind of like being wise.

Was Arete right? Should she, too, consider ditching her friendship with Glauce? It was definitely toxic and often upsetting. But could it truly be that easy?

"Okay, well, the real reason I came over is I just wanted to say that I hope you're going to try out for Magicasters," said Arete.

Medea shook her head. "I wish. But since I don't board, I wouldn't be able to make the meetings."

Seeing another friend waving to her, Arete gobbled the last few bites of her food. Then, giving Medea a quick, friendly smile, she stood to go. "Just try out," she coaxed. "If you can stay after school today, just this once, I mean. Then we'll worry about you making the meetings later."

As Medea watched Arete head out of the cafeteria with the other girl, a new thought occurred to her. *If my friendship with Glauce is one of the things I should* undo, *maybe tryouts are one of the things I should do.* Thinking hard on this, she stood to go to the tray return.

Glauce popped up at the same moment and followed with her own tray. "Buddying up to one of the Magicasters Club members?" she asked.

Medea shrugged. "Arete, you mean? We were just talking about tryouts."

"No offense, but you really shouldn't try out for the Magicasters if you haven't been practicing for it. I mean, it's not something you just up and do. I've been perfecting my act for ages. I'm only saying this for your own good. Don't forget the tomato incident. Imagine doing something that embarrassing during tryouts in front of a whole auditorium!"

Medea seethed with anger at Glauce's seemingly deliberate attempt to undermine her confidence. Instead of imagining what Glauce wanted her to, she imagined her eyes flashing so hotly that they blasted Glauce and her sly remarks to smithereens! But then she thought of Arete. Would that girl have taken Glauce's bait in this situation and gotten jealous? No! Not anymore, Arete wouldn't. And neither would *she*, Medea decided.

So she just shrugged and said pleasantly, "Thanks for the advice, but I am going to try out. Good luck at the auditions."

At her calm, confident reply Glauce's head jerked back and dismay filled her face. Medea's response was obviously not the reaction she'd wanted or expected.

"And, no offense," Medea said, purposely using Glauce's own phrase, "but I wish you wouldn't say things to me for 'my own good.' I can decide for myself what is or isn't good for me."

Hmph. "You sure?" Glauce replied snidely.

"Actually, yes. I am *totally* sure," Medea said firmly. Feeling much lighter, she walked away from

Glauce and maybe from a toxic friendship, too.

At the school's office Medea sent word to her dad back in Colchis that she had an after-school project and hoped he'd understand that she'd be home late, maybe not till after sundown. Then, for the rest of the day, she tried to think of an act to perform at tryouts. She had talked big, but now she had to do something big. If she'd had more time to talk herself out of trying out, she might have. But she was filled with annoyance-at-Glauce-inspired confidence.

Afternoon classes flew by. Before she knew it, Medea was walking into the open-air auditorium for Magicasters tryouts. Every contestant had brought a "bag of tricks," which was basically a schoolbag containing whatever props they'd need for their audition. The seventeen other students trying out had probably planned what to bring, but Medea had just randomly pulled things from her locker that might come in handy. All too soon, the judges announced that they would each be allotted ten minutes to perform an "original, awe-inspiring act of magic" that showcased their special skills.

The magic skills on display proved to be amazing. One girl used her magic to blow out the auditorium's torches and make everyone's teeth glow in the dark. A boy changed the judges into monkeys. It was only for five seconds, but they didn't seem happy about it, so maybe his trick hadn't been the best idea, actually.

And then Glauce did her act. It was a stunner. She magicked up a life-size image of Jason and had him blow kisses to the crowd! A wave of girls' sighs cascaded over the audience at how cute he was.

After Glauce sat down, Medea felt a moment of doubt. The other contestants were so talented.

How could she ever compete? She'd been trying to think of an idea for today's tryouts ever since she'd talked with Arete at lunch. She didn't really have a special talent she was proud of. Only one she *wasn't* proud of.

She sat up straighter in her seat. Hey, maybe . . . could she use her eye-flash curse, um, *ability* in her act? Did she dare? Practically the whole school had gathered to watch these tryouts. What if she fried the entire club, the judges, and everyone in the audience? That was a shudder-worthy thought!

Ever since Glauce had teased her about her eye-flash power in first grade, she had tried to squash it and hide it away somewhere deep inside her. Like putting it in a prison. And only when she grew angry was it able to burst out of that prison. But what if she stopped holding it captive? What if she let it out in an orderly, positive way that didn't harm anyone? A way that only helped others. The notion was as intriguing to her as it was new.

She would need a good idea to showcase her so-called talent. Something that would wow (but not horrify!) the judges. As the other contestants continued taking turns performing, Medea racked her brain for a way to make her eye-flash talent shine. From a few rows back she could hear Glauce bragging to another girl about one of the letters she'd gotten from Jason. "He's so sweet. Did I tell you he said my hair is like the sun and my eyes are like stars?"

Hearing this, Medea smiled to herself. Because suddenly she knew what she would do. When it was finally her turn to try out, the last of the contestants as it happened, she climbed boldly onto the stage with her schoolbag in hand.

"You may begin in your own time, but remember you have only ten minutes," one of the judges told her as soon as she stood onstage before them. Seventeen contestants had gone before her, and night had fallen. The auditorium's many torches glowed softly in the darkness. Perfect. Quickly Medea set down her bag, then pulled her wand and a small hand mirror out of it, before straightening again to face the crowd. Holding the mirror reflective side up in one palm, she took a deep breath and closed her eyes.

She didn't rush her special fry-power or try to imprison it either. And for once she didn't summon anger in order to set it free. Instead she tried to call up her talent with a determination born of the new confidence she felt in herself. To her surprise, she felt her power begin to rise within her in a controlled sort of way. Slowly and surely she let it build . . . and build, until it was strong enough to travel to places farther than she'd ever sent her magic before. Did she dare? Thoughts of the tomato incident tried to creep in and undermine her confidence. No! She pushed them away, keeping her concentration.

When Medea felt ready, she slowly opened her eyes and looked down to view the image reflected in her mirror—that of the star-filled heavens high above her. Holding her wand in the most precise position, fifth, she carefully touched its gold tip to the surface of the mirror. *Tap!* With all her might she focused the power of her gaze and sent it hurtling into the mirror, where it was then bounced high overhead into the night sky. On the mirror's surface, she watched pin dots of light magically rearrange themselves.

After a few silent moments she lifted her eyes to gaze out at the judges. She smiled. "All finished," she announced.

The judges and students in the crowd glanced around curiously, not understanding. "But what did you do?" one of the judges finally asked.

Medea raised one finger, pointing up and directing everyone's attention toward the heavens. Amazed and delighted gasps rippled across the auditorium as everyone saw what she'd done. One by one, bright pinpoints of light were appearing overhead, forming a pattern of new stars among those already in the night sky.

"In honor of Jason and the Argonauts, I have created a constellation in the shape of their ship, the *Argo*," Medea explained once the stars had settled.

"From now on it will be visible each night in the springtime sky. And as the Earth rotates, the star ship will appear to sail westward, skimming along the southern horizon of the Mediterranean Sea, just as Jason's ship did. It will be known as Argo Navis, the biggest constellation in the sky."

There was a moment of stunned silence as all in the auditorium took in the enormity of the act she had just performed. Then applause broke out, loud and long. For her! And her talent!

Even if she didn't win, Medea felt happy. Exhilarated, in fact. And proud. Her constellation would forever and ever serve as a reminder to everyone of the *Argo*'s remarkable voyage. On clear nights, anyway.

The judges put their heads together and swiftly reached a decision. "Your project has out*shone* all

the rest. Welcome to the Magicasters Club, Medea!"
Next, they announced two new members, neither of
whom was Glauce.

Out in the crowd Arete sent Medea an excited
thumbs-up, but Glauce looked sour.

Suddenly Medea realized something. That maybe
Glauce had been jealous of *her* all along. Was that why
she'd always stuck close, yet spent all her time putting
Medea down? To keep Medea from rising . . . from
shining? Medea knew how jealousy could eat away at
a person—how it had eaten away at her for years!

She felt kind of sorry for Glauce now that she
understood, but she also felt *free*. Because she'd figured out what was what, so Glauce couldn't hurt her
ever again.

12

Enchantment Academy

WE NEED TO TALK," MEDEA'S DAD TOLD HER when she got home from school that night. Though he didn't sound mad at her, she held her breath. Had he not gotten her message saying she would be late? Was she about to be punished for breaking the rule about coming home from school right away?

For a few moments he paced back and forth on the long, fancy carpet runner that led up to his throne.

Finally he paused to stand before her. "I've been doing some thinking about your *Argo* adventure, Medea. You proved you can take care of yourself and make good decisions in difficult circumstances. So I've decided that you can board at Enchantment Academy during the school year from now on. I've talked it over with your aunt Circe, and she has agreed to keep an eye out for you. But you'll come home every other weekend and during summers. Deal?"

Medea could hardly believe it. "Deal!" Her dad smiled when she began hopping around with excitement. Then she did something she hadn't done in a long time. She gave him the biggest hug ever. "Thanks, Dad!"

"No prob," he said, making her laugh. When she talked slang like that, he usually corrected her. Maybe he'd decided to relax some of his other rules too. Things between them were looking up. Hooray!

The next morning, earlier than usual, Circe transported Medea, her book bag, and a large suitcase to EA so she could get settled in her new dorm room. She would be sharing, like all the other students at the school. Her roommate wasn't in when she arrived. Which probably meant that she was at breakfast or taking a shower down the hall.

There were two desks, so Medea set her stuff on top of the empty one. Then she peeked at her roommate's desk curiously. Her heart leaped when she saw that the name *Arete* was written on a papyrus sheet of schoolwork. *Woo-hoo!* Medea did a happy dance on the rug in the center of the room. What luck to get Arete as her roommate! They'd be in Magicasters together and could practice magic stuff!

She stopped dancing when something flew in

through the open window and landed on her new bed. It was this week's issue of *Teen Scrollazine*! With her name on it! There was a note attached to it:

DEAR MEDEA,

AS A NEW-DORM-ROOM GIFT FOR YOU,

I HAVE GOTTEN YOU A SUBSCRIPTION

TO THAT 'ZINE YOU LIKE. I MISS YOU

ALREADY AND LOOK FORWARD TO SEEING

YOU THIS WEEKEND. I AM SO PROUD OF

THE RESPONSIBLE, GROWN-UP GIRL YOU

ARE BECOMING.

LOVE,

DAD

With a sigh of contentment, Medea hugged the scrollazine to her chest. Right away she flopped down on her bed to lie on her stomach. She flicked her wand's gold tip at the 'zine, like she was conducting a band of musicians. *Whoosh!* The 'zine unrolled before her, atop her bedcovers.

She sucked in her breath when she discovered that the lead article was the very first installment of Pheme's story about the *Argo*'s adventures. Classes would begin in an hour, she still had stuff to put away, and there would be greetings to exchange with Arete. But all that could wait for a bit. Tuning out the world, she began to read.

Wary at first, her feelings soon turned to delight when she saw that Pheme had done her research. Her article presented the true and actual facts of the voyage, not a made-up story colored to suit Glauce. Soon everyone would know the truth of Medea's role in helping Jason to capture the fleece. Cool!

There was a side story about Heracles, too. Apparently, he had found his way back to Mount Olympus Academy. He never did find Hylas, but Eros had managed to remove the crushing spell that made him adore that shield, so all was well.

At the bottom of the sidebar was a message from Pheme to her readers saying that future articles would include interviews with other Hero-ology students about their actions during the quest and their views on what happened. Fun! Medea would love to learn what they had to say about the quest.

Not only that, at the end of the main article there was a note that the musical based on Orpheus's and Apollonius's co-written story was already in rehearsals. It was scheduled to open at the end of the year at the Theatre of Dionysus, below the Acropolis in Greece. One way or another she would find a way to go see it, Medea thought excitedly. And since many of the MOA students she'd met would no doubt attend too, she'd get to see them again. She could hardly wait!

Looking up from her 'zine, Medea glanced around her new room. A warm feeling spread through her as she took in her tiny wardrobe and desk and the drawing she'd made of the *Argo*, which she'd already tacked onto the wall beside her bed. She didn't need a prophecy from Aunt Circe to predict that the months ahead were going to make this her . . . Best! Year! *Ever!*

Goddess Girls

READ ABOUT ALL
YOUR FAVORITE GODDESSES!

**#16 MEDUSA
THE RICH**

**#17 AMPHITRITE
THE BUBBLY**

**#18 HESTIA
THE INVISIBLE**

**#19 ECHO
THE COPYCAT**

**#20 CALLIOPE
THE MUSE**

**#21 PALLAS
THE PAL**

**#22 NYX
THE MYSTERIOUS**

**#23 MEDEA
THE ENCHANTRESS**

EBOOK EDITIONS ALSO AVAILABLE

From Aladdin
simonandschuster.com/kids

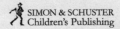